AVALANCHE OF DESIRE
BROTHERS FREED – BOOK ONE

BEA PAIGE

To Laura
Luv
Bea Paige
xx

Avalanche of Desire

Brothers Freed – Book one

UK ENGLISH AND SLANG KEY

This book has been written by a British author who uses UK British spellings and slang. Please see a list below of those words and phrases that may be unfamiliar or confusing to non-native Brits.

A&E – short for Accident & Emergency, US equivalent of ER

'Bunged-up' – when you have a cold or flu and you can't breathe, sinuses / airways are full of fluid

Eiderdown – A quilt, often filled with feathers

'Full-stop' – ending a sentence with the phrase 'full-stop' basically means you have never or will never do something. In this case - *We didn't do Christmas full stop.*

Holdall – same as a suitcase, a bag that carries personal belongings

Paracetamol – British branded painkiller for headaches, aches and pains

Plait - braid

'Shed load' – means 'a lot'

'Sterling job' – sterling means very good in quality, so if you do a 'sterling job', you've done something well

'Taking the piss' – making fun out of something, someone

Tannoy – a public address system

For the men who exist inside my head, thanks for all the entertainment.

ONE

"Louisa! Get your arse down here, NOW!"

Sighing, I pick up my bag and coat and head into the living room. Sitting on the sofa is my mum and snuggled up next to her a rather drunk Dom, or Fred, or whatever the hell this new client, I mean *boyfriend*, is called. "What is it, Mum?" I ask, trying not to notice that Dom has his hand up her top.

"We need more booze. Do us a favour and go grab us a bottle of vodka from the off-licence." Noticing the look of disgust on my face, she pushes Dom's hand away.

"Oy, not in front of Louisa. She's a prude." The sound of her laugh sets my teeth on edge.

"I'm not a prude. I just don't think it's appropriate to be all over each other like a couple of teenagers while I'm in the room."

Mum looks at me, her eyes bloodshot. "You're twenty-two, Louisa, isn't it about time you got yourself a fella? Might loosen you up a bit."

"I don't *need* a boyfriend. I don't *need* loosening up. I

5

need a mother who actually gives a shit about me. I need a mother who doesn't spend her whole existence getting pissed and shagging the next bloke for a few quid!"

Mum pushes Dom off her and attempts to stand, but she is so drunk she only manages to fall forward onto the coffee table, ending up on her arse on the floor. I stay where I am, too angry to help.

"Don't you look down your nose at me!" she screams from her spot on the floor. "You're lucky you got a home to live in, girl. Now make yourself useful and go get me some fucking vodka!"

I sigh and hold my hand out for the money whilst Dom heaves her off the floor. For as long as I can remember she's been a drunk. My real father left us when I was a toddler and her drinking has gotten steadily worse over the years. Her addiction isn't helped by the fact that she always has a stream of so-called boyfriends who seem to encourage her bad habits; drinking and being a shitty mother are two of her worst. There was only one man who almost turned my mother around, but she ruined that relationship too, just like she ruins everything else. I am still in touch with Richard, he hasn't abandoned me even though he gave up on my mother five years ago. In fact, I am on my way to visit him now. He has a job opportunity that he thought I might be interested in, and given I am broke and in desperate need of cash, I agreed to hear him out.

When I look at my mum now, sitting in her stained tracksuit, her blonde hair greasy and her skin tinged grey, I am reminded that I will never have the mother I always wanted. Before the alcohol ravaged her looks, she had been

6

attractive, beautiful even. In her sober moments, she would tell me that I looked just like her when she was my age and would brag that I was even better looking. I miss my lucid mum, but she isn't around much anymore. Whether I like it or not, the woman before me is all I have.

"Are you alright, Mum?" I sigh.

"*Now* the fucking sympathy. Just take the money and piss off," she screeches.

Dom leers at me, his own eyes hazy and unfocused. "That's a good girl. Do what Mummy says," he titters, blowing cigarette smoke at me. I want to smack the look off his face, but I don't. I take the money and leave.

———

"Louisa, love, it's good to see you," Richard says as I enter the café, mum's bottle of vodka in my hand. "That for Lorna?" he asks, pointing to the bottle.

I place it on the Formica table and shrug off my winter jacket. "No, it's mine," I say sarcastically, pulling off my beanie hat and scarf, my blonde hair tumbling free.

"Stupid question." He smiles kindly at me and I feel guilty for being such a bitch. "Rough day?"

"You know what Mum's like. She's got herself a new boyfriend, and she's worse than ever. She's so pissed right now that I doubt she'll even remember asking me to buy her this bottle of vodka."

Richard looks at me with a worried expression on his ruggedly handsome face. He is a couple of years older than mum, who's forty-nine, though she looks far older. I never understood why Mum made him leave. He had been good for her, for us, and the only man who ever really gave a shit about her. Mum tolerates our friendship, when she is bothered enough to stay relatively sober, that is. Otherwise, she curses both me and Richard for all her problems. Most days his name is mud, just like mine.

"If I thought I could help her get dry, Louisa, I would..." His voice trails off as the waitress arrives with a cappuccino for Richard and a latte for me.

"Thanks," I mumble.

"Can I get you anything else?" the waitress asks.

"That's it for now," Richard says. She leaves us in peace and I take a sip of my drink.

"So, you said you might have some work for me?"

"You know the offer still stands, Louisa," Richard says, ignoring my question for the moment. "You can come live with me if it gets too much." He pats my hand, and it's all I can do to stop myself from bursting into tears. I don't look at his face, I can't. His kindness and his friendship have been the only things that have kept me sane these last five years.

"She's my mum, Richard. Despite everything she's done to me, I can't leave her."

Richard sighs. "I understand, Louisa, truly I do. But she's a grown woman. She must take responsibility for herself. It isn't up to you to fix her. You can't do that, love."

I press my fingers against my eyes. "I know, but I have to try."

Richard gives me a moment to gather myself, then slides a holiday brochure onto the table. On the front of it is a picture of a ski slope with people dressed in colourful skiwear. They are all smiling. I look at him with a frown.

"What's this?"

"This is what I was talking about. I've been working as the marketing director for a ski resort in Alpe d'Huez, France. My friend Bastien is running the resort. One of the chalet girls has had to go home, and he needs to replace her fast. He owes me a favour, so I called it in. I asked if he would hire you for the job."

My mouth drops open. "That's the work you were talking about? But…"

Richard holds his hand up. "Don't rule it out just yet, let me tell you about it first."

"I can't possibly go. You heard what I said about Mum. Besides, Christmas is three weeks away. You know what happened to Mum last year," I say, shaking my head. I glance at the brochure again wishing, not for the first time, that I had a mother who isn't a deadbeat drunk. I am tired of the role-reversal.

"Hear me out, Louisa. That's all I ask."

"Fine," I say, but I know I won't take the job. Every Christmas Mum loses her shit. Last year was by far the worst. She'd gone on a bender for a week and was taken to A&E after some little old lady found her unconscious at the local park, covered in cuts and bruises. The police thought she had drunk too much and passed out, knocking her head. But I saw the marks on her skin and I knew that more had happened to her. It was the only time I thanked God she was a drunk, at least she wouldn't have remembered anything.

"The job starts next week and will run through to the new

year, longer if you want to stay until the end of the season. Flights are covered, and you will stay the whole duration in the chalet your guests will be holidaying in. You will need to provide breakfast and dinner for your guests, tidy their rooms, that kind of stuff. But between the hours of ten thirty am and five pm you're free to do as you please. Most other staff spend their time skiing. Once the evening meal is finished and you've tidied up, the rest of the night is your own. What do you say, Louisa?"

I look from Richard's eager face to the brochure and back again. It sounds so wonderful. The thought of spending a whole month away from my mum and her shitty 'boyfriends' is so tempting. I've never been abroad before, let alone out of London, so the thought of living in a beautiful wooden chalet nestled in the hills of some snowy mountain is like a dream come true. Yet I push the brochure back to Richard.

"You know I can't."

"Louisa…" Richard starts, just as my phone begins to ring. I look at the screen. It's Mum. I swipe across and press my ear to the phone.

"Where the bloody hell are you? Dom and I have been waiting for fucking ages. Bring us the damn drink you useless, good for nothing piece of sh..."

I don't bother to listen to the rest of the call. I hang up and grab the brochure from Richard, who is about to put it back in his bag.

"What time's the flight?" I ask.

TWO

"Here are your tickets. Bastien has arranged for one of the other chalet girls to pick you up from Grenoble airport when you land. Her name is Shawna, I believe," Richard says, handing me the documents I need to get on the plane.

"Thanks," I mumble, not able to express my true gratitude. To be honest, I am completely overwhelmed. The last few days have been a whirlwind of packing and making arrangements for my trip away. At first, when I told Mum of my plans she had been adamant that I shouldn't go, that I was being a selfish brat, but when I explained how much money I would earn to send home to her she soon gave me her blessing. Frankly, I don't care what she uses the money for. I just need to get away, if only for a short while.

"You are doing the right thing, Louisa. It's about time you think of yourself. I'll pop in on your mum from time to time, okay. Don't worry about what happens here." Richard pulls me in for a quick hug before planting a kiss on my head. Overhead the tannoy sounds and my flight is called.

"Thanks for everything, Richard," I say, a lump forming in my throat.

"You're very welcome. Now go on, go. Have fun, Louisa."

"I'll call in a few days to see how things are."

"I look forward to it," Richard says, before walking away.

I watch him leave through the sliding glass doors then pick up my handbag and luggage and make my way towards check-in, feeling equally excited and anxious. When I finally get to the front of the queue a British Airways attendant flashes me a beautiful smile. She is young, probably my age, and very pretty with dark hair, brown eyes and long dark lashes.

"Are you checking in on your own?" she asks.

"Yes. I'm going to be a chalet girl," I blurt out.

"That sounds great, I always fancied a job like that with all those hunky ski instructors. How romantic, all that snow outside and warm, open fires inside," she says, sighing dramatically.

"Oh, I hadn't really thought about that. I'm just happy to be getting on an aeroplane for the first time." It's true, I haven't thought beyond the flight. If I'm totally honest, I am a little nervous, it being my first time flying. It didn't help that just before I left, my mother decided to fill me in on all the plane crashes that have happened over the years.

"Is that so," the attendant says, considering me for a moment. "Well, it just so happens to be your lucky day. You've been upgraded to business class."

I look at her incredulously. "Wait, what? Oh no, it's okay. I don't have any money for that."

She grins. "Don't worry, it's a complimentary upgrade. Enjoy your first flight on a plane," she says as she sticks a label on my luggage. "You can go through to the departure lounge now."

"Thank you," I say, shaking my head in disbelief.

"That's quite alright, Miss Budd. Have fun with the ski instructors and don't do anything I wouldn't do." She winks, handing me back my passport.

A few minutes later I am through the security check and heading towards Costa in the departure lounge. There is a separate sign showing the way to the business class area, but I don't bother following it. Instead, I make myself comfortable with my latte, muffin and Cosmopolitan magazine and before long it's time to board.

"Welcome on board. Your seat is through here and to the right," the air stewardess says politely.

"Thanks." I take my ticket from her and search for my seat. Business class is separated by a curtain partition and I can see that the seats in this section of the plane are roomier than the standard ones. I have a window seat rather than an aisle, and I'm glad because I can't wait to look out of the window to view the scenery. After storing my coat and handbag in the overhead compartment, I sit down.

"Jesus, Max, can you not give it a rest for one minute?"

I look up to see a ridiculously handsome man with short, dark brown hair and the greenest eyes I've ever seen stop at the end of the row I'm sitting in. He's talking to a blonde-haired guy who is taking a seat in the row opposite.

"Never, man. Why would I? You saw the way she looked at me. Looks like I'll be joining the mile-high club today," Blondie says, chuckling.

"Leave him alone, Hudson," another guy says as he smacks green-eyes on the back. He's a huge beast of a man and all the more attractive for it. "You're only pissed because you didn't get in there first."

"As if, Bryce," green-eyes snorts. "As the eldest, you know as well as I do that I always get first dibs on the ladies. She just wasn't my type." He turns his back on the laughing men and opens the overhead locker. Realising it's full, he opens the next one along and stashes his holdall away. I watch him as he removes his thick, cable-knit sweater, revealing a glimpse of defined stomach muscles covered in a smattering of dark hair. I look away quickly, not wishing to be caught ogling him.

Now that green-eyes is no longer blocking my view, I can get a good look at the other men he boarded with. They don't look much like brothers to me, but I guess just because you share blood it doesn't mean you have to be the image of each other. The man-mountain is taller than green-eyes, the other, Blondie, slightly shorter. They both have the same tanned skin like they've been on a year-long holiday. Blondie, the one I think they called Max, has dark brown eyes and well-styled hair, long on top and cropped at the sides, whilst the man-mountain has dark black hair pulled back in a bun and is sporting a well-groomed beard. His eyes are hazel. Mountain-man catches me staring and gives me a wink, a sexy smile lingering on his lips.

I look down at my magazine, pretending to read, thankful that my long hair can shield my embarrassment. A moment later, Green-eyes takes a seat next to me. He coughs, and I look up.

"You might want to do that up," he says, pointing to my lap.

I look down, expecting to see my flies undone, then frown when I don't understand what he's talking about. "Sorry?" I say.

He gives me a questioning look then leans over, grabbing a seatbelt I hadn't noticed until that moment. I press my back into the chair, shocked by his sudden nearness. He smells of expensive aftershave and danger.

"There," he says, clicking it together. "You're all strapped in and ready for take-off."

"You could have just told me," I snap, pissed that he thinks he can just get into my personal space like that. I don't know why I react that way. It's not often you get an attractive man strapping you into a seat, but something about his presumptuousness pisses me off.

He looks at me, eyebrows knotting together as if he didn't expect that response. Then he shakes himself and holds out his hand. "My name's Hudson. Those two imbeciles over there are my younger brothers, Max and Bryce," he says, pointing at them. I glance over, and they are both grinning inanely at us. "Ignore them, they have huge egos. They think they're God's gift to women."

"And you? Do you think you're God's gift to women?" I ask before I can stop myself.

Hudson looks at me, the easy smile dropping from his face, replaced instead with something far sexier. "You tell me," he says.

I look at his ridiculously handsome face and suddenly have the urge to knock him down a peg or two. He is way too cocky for my liking. "I think you and your brothers are very alike. Big egos appear to run in your family, no?"

Hudson's eyes widen as his brothers laugh loudly. I smile inwardly, feeling I've handled the situation pretty well, considering.

For the rest of the flight, Hudson doesn't bother talking to me again. Instead, he chooses to spend the entire time chatting up another air stewardess. Frankly, I don't give two shits. After I get off this flight, I won't be seeing either Hudson or his brothers again.

THREE

"Hey, you must be Louisa. I'm Shawna, pleased to meet you." A tall girl, about my age, with long brown hair and speckled green and brown eyes, holds out her hand to greet me. I go to shake it, but she pulls me into a hug. "Don't be silly, we're not that formal here," she says, laughing. "Now, where's your bag? Let's dump it in the car and get going."

I watch as she pinches her finger and thumb together, puts them in her mouth and whistles. A minute later a black 4x4 pulls up and a man with bronzed skin and white blonde hair gets out. He looks like he should be surfing on a beach, not here in the below freezing weather of the French Alps.

"This is Pierre, he's my boyfriend," Shawna says. She passes him my bag and whispers in my ear, "He's a dream in bed. Like, *super* sexy."

"Bonjour, c'est un plaisir de vous rencontrer. Bienvenue en France. Je suis votre chauffeur," Pierre says as he puts my suitcase in the boot of the car. I look at Shawna and grimace.

"I have no idea what he just said."

Shawna laughs. "Nope, me neither, but isn't it just so damn *hot?*" She leans in and gives Pierre a passionate kiss. I look away and take in the scenery about me. The air is crisp, and my breath comes out in smoky puffs. Although the roads are clear, the sidings and rooftops of the nearby buildings are covered in a thick layer of powdery snow. The sky itself is grey and full of heavy billowing clouds. In the distance, I can see the white peaks of mountains and wonder whether that's where we are heading.

"We're due to get some snow later today, so we'd better get a move on if we don't want to get stuck in it. Pierre's a great ski instructor but driving, not so much," Shawna says, pulling a face.

"How long will it take to get to the resort?" I ask as I slide into the back of the car. Shawna climbs in next to me whilst Pierre starts the engine.

"An hour or so with Pierre's driving. He's a bit of a speed freak. Plus, he wants to get back for après-ski."

"What's après-ski?" I ask, clicking my seat belt in. For a second I am reminded of Green-eyes, and how he took it upon himself to strap me in on the plane. Now that I think about it, his behaviour was really bloody cocky. He's the type of bloke who always has a stream of lovers at his beck and call, and entirely the kind of man I avoid like the plague. Thank fuck he and his brothers went on their merry way somewhere else. Pushing thoughts of the three brothers aside I turn to Shawna, waiting for her answer.

"You don't know what après-ski is?" Shawna's mouth drops open, and she gives me a 'you've got to be kidding' look. "It's only *the* best part of the day. All the instructors, chalet girls, locals, holidaymakers, we all get together and basically party the night away. You must come, I can introduce you to everyone. It'll be a blast!"

I look at Shawna warily. "Don't I have to get the chalet ready for the family that's staying? I mean, I don't want to mess up on my first night here."

Pierre pulls out into the traffic, making a sharp turn onto the connecting motorway.

"Oh, didn't I say? Your family isn't arriving until late tomorrow night. Apparently, they're stopping off in the city before heading to the resort. So, you're free!" she sings.

I laugh, her enthusiasm is catching. To be honest, I am not much of a drinker; Mum has put me off booze for life, but just the one drink couldn't hurt. "Alright then, just for a bit," I say.

"Awesome!"

For the rest of the drive, I sit and listen to Shawna chatter about life at the resort. She arrived a month ago, met Pierre the first week and, apparently, they have been inseparable ever since.

"I mean, he's just the most amazing lover, Louisa, huge co-" Shawna spreads her hands wide, pulling a face. I can't help but giggle.

"When I first saw it I was like, what am I supposed to do with *that*? Though it didn't take me long to get used to it!"

I can't quite believe that Shawna is telling me about her sex life. It's pretty surreal, given Pierre is sitting in front of us, seemingly ignorant of our conversation. Girls talk about their men, I know that, but not normally right in front of them. I tip my head towards Pierre and pull a face. Shawna laughs.

"Oh, don't worry about Pierre. His English is a bit on the rusty side. He can converse enough to instruct but otherwise, nope. It's just as well, really, because we spend most of our time shagging anyway. How about you, any boyfriends back home?"

"Not for a while," I say. "The last boyfriend I had dropped me as soon as he met my mother. It wasn't a planned meeting, she just happened to come into the pub we were in one night. A half-assed attempt at giving my boyfriend a lap dance then puking on his jeans pretty much ended our relationship."

"Ah, fuck. Your mum's like that, huh?"

I shrug my shoulders. "Yeah, pretty much."

"Well look, you not having a boyfriend is pretty perfect, actually. You'll meet loads of hot men at the resort. Just you wait until later. I hope you've brought some clubbing outfits."

I pull a face; getting away from my mother's grasp had been foremost on my mind, clubbing not so much. My suitcase is packed full of thermal underwear, winter clothes, and thick, woolly jumpers. None of which are suitable for clubbing.

"Don't worry about it. I have plenty of stuff you can borrow. Once you've unpacked and settled in, I'll come to yours with a couple of outfits. We can get ready together."

"Um, okay then," I say, too polite to decline her offer. I don't really go clubbing or dress up for that matter. I'm a jeans and t-shirt kind of girl.

"That's settled then," Shawna says, unhooking her seat belt and pointing to the front of the car. "Do you mind?"

"Sure," I say.

A moment later she's climbing into the front seat and chatting to Pierre. I am fascinated with how they converse, seeing as neither of them appears to know what the other is saying but are happy in each other's company, nonetheless. I watch how they keep touching each other as though they cannot bear to be without physical contact. That kind of closeness is completely alien to me. I mean, I've had sex before, yes. But frankly, it wasn't anything to write home about. A quick fumble, then a *wham bam, thank you, Ma'am,* is about the extent of my sexual experience. Basically, all my previous lovers were dicks who, funnily enough, thought with their dicks. I sigh and spend the rest of the journey watching the scenery roll by as the mountains of Alpe d'Huez loom larger the nearer we get.

It isn't much longer until we reach the resort. Pierre stops outside a beautiful wooden chalet that's three times the size of my terrace house back home. We had to drive through the resort to get to it, and it is set back from all the other chalets, which are further down the hill and closer to the centre of the resort. It is surrounded by alpine trees covered in a layer of snow, their branches straining under the weight of it. The chalet has a wraparound porch and large glass windows on the ground floor. There are covered balconies on the upper floors, all of which have a thick layer of snow settled upon them. The nearest chalet is at least five hundred yards away. It is beautiful, secluded, but close enough to the slopes to be in a prime location.

21

"This is you," Shawna says, jumping out of the car.

I look up at the chalet in amazement, my breath steaming up the window. Pierre opens the door then holds his arm out, grinning at the stunned look on my face.

"This is where I'll be staying?" I say, gobsmacked.

Shawna laughs. "Yup, you've got the high end of the market. This is a four double-bed chalet with sauna, steam room and pool. It's stunning. I mean, I'm pretty jealous right about now."

"There must be some kind of mistake. Why would they give me this chalet? I'm new, I might mess it up." Worry threads through me at the possibility that I am in over my head. I mean, clearly, whoever has paid to stay in this chalet must have a lot of money and therefore probably has high expectations of their chalet girl. I can cook okay, and clean, but I am no chef.

"Don't be daft. You just need to make sure you keep the place tidy, cook a good fry up and sort out the evening meal. Come on up," Shawna says, climbing the steps to the front porch. She points to the case and Pierre picks it up for me. I puff out my cheeks and breathe out slowly, following them through the front door.

The inside of the chalet is just as lovely as the outside and it is as big as I imagined it would be. The whole ground floor is open plan, with a stainless-steel kitchen taking up one side, and a beautifully decorated sitting room with an open fire, a chocolate brown L-shaped sofa and oversized armchair on the other. The warm wood of the kitchen table and chairs complement the wooden walls and floor of the chalet, making the place feel welcoming and cosy.

"Right, well, here you are. Pierre and I are going to shoot off. Your room is in the basement next to the pool. As accommodation goes us chalet girls don't get anything near as nice as what you've got down there. If I were you, I would totally make use of all the good stuff before your family arrives. Oh, and your room has an en-suite. You've totally lucked out, girl. Let's just hope the family you get aren't arseholes!" Shawna laughs, gives me a brief hug then pulls on Pierre's hand. "Come on, let's leave Louisa to settle in." She turns to me briefly and smiles. "We're going back to mine for a bit. I'll be back later, at about eight. I'll bring you something to wear. You look about my size." She pulls me into a brief hug then leaves, Pierre in tow.

I lean against the door and let the beauty of the chalet sink in. This place just about exceeds all my expectations, and I have a good four hours until Shawna returns. Time to check out the rest of the place. I let out a delighted squeal, all thoughts of home pushed firmly out of my mind.

FOUR

I sit in my dressing gown, watching Shawna pull out a variety of skimpy outfits and chuck them on the bed next to me.

"How about this one? I love this dress. I pulled Pierre in it," she says, holding up what appears to be two silver hankies tied together with string.

"Um, I think I might be a bit cold in that one," I say diplomatically. Frankly, I would look like a slut, but I don't want to hurt her feelings. Despite what she said earlier, I am a little shapelier than her lean figure. Basically, I had tits and an arse, and I'd be falling out all over the place in that skimpy number.

"Hmm, I see what you mean. Although the club gets pretty steamy, you only really need your ski jacket to throw over you until you're inside. Then you'll be thanking me for making you wear something like this."

"What about my legs?" I ask.

"What about your legs?" Shawna laughs. "You'll get used to the cold, I promise."

"Sure I will," I say, not at all convinced.

"So, what *are* you going to wear then? If you want to pull, thermal underwear and jeans just aren't going to cut it." She taps her finger against her cheek, looking thoughtful. "Oh, I know. How about this t-shirt, and this mini skirt?"

I take my Pink Floyd t-shirt from her and shake my head at the mini skirt. "I'll wear this t-shirt, with these," I say, picking up some black, fake leather skinny jeans. They are the only thing she's brought that is remotely normal looking. "And those," I say, pointing to my trusty pair of biker boots.

She considers the outfit for a moment. "Well, I suppose it is sexy in a rock-chick kind of way. Hell, why not? But don't blame me when you turn into a sweaty mess. You have been warned."

I pull on the clothes whilst Shawna makes herself at home, sniffing my perfume and looking through the small amount of makeup I've brought with me. I smudge on some kohl eyeliner to highlight my blue eyes, add a dash of lip gloss and I am done.

"What do you think?" I ask.

Shawna grins. "The boys are going to love you! God, I wished I could pull off a look like that. It totally suits you. You're like Debbie Harry, although a thousand times better looking."

"Thanks, I think."

Before heading to the club, we stop off at Shawna's place for an hour to have a few glasses of red wine and to pick up a ski

26

pass she forgot to give me earlier. I take it, but don't tell her that I'm not planning on doing any skiing. I can barely walk on the snow, let alone ski on it.

Another ten, treacherous minutes' walk later we arrive at Le Carnaval club. It is not dissimilar to the other surrounding buildings, the only defining difference is a large neon sign that flashes red against the wooden façade. Out front is a large seating area where a load of people are congregating, drinking and smoking. Shawna spots Pierre and pulls me along. I try not to fall on my arse in front of the crowd.

"Hey everyone, this is Louisa, she's staying in the Palace at the top of the hill."

I hear a chorus of hellos before they all turn back to their conversations.

"Palace?" I ask Shawna, but she's already gone over to a group of girls and is animatedly chatting away. They laugh, and I wonder whether she is telling them stories about her sex life. They are pretty amusing.

"That's what the locals call it because it's so posh," a guy with smiling blue eyes says. He holds out his hand. "I'm Luke, good to meet you."

I take his hand and shake it. "Nice to meet you too," I say, but it comes out sounding weird because my teeth are chattering so much. He laughs.

"You'll acclimatise soon enough. Want to go inside?"

"Sure," I say. I give a little wave to Shawna and she gives me the thumbs up.

Inside, the club is a hell of a lot warmer than outside and it doesn't take long for me to regret wearing fake leather trousers. After putting my coat in the cloakroom, Luke takes me to the bar and orders us both a pint of local beer. I don't actually like beer, but I am too polite to refuse it and murmur my thanks instead. We sit on the barstools, chatting small talk and watching the crowd. He's nice, but not really my type. For the next half an hour, he tells me how he arrived at the same time as Shawna, that he has been coming to the resort every year for the last five years and that there are no better slopes to ski on, in his opinion. I nod my head and smile at all the right times but find myself losing interest pretty quickly. While he drones on about the different slopes and their difficulty grades, my attention turns to the club interior.

The lighting in the club is dim, and the dance floor is already heaving with scantily clad girls and sweaty men. There are swathes of red material hanging from the ceiling in folds, like the roof of a circus. In each corner there are dancers dressed in outfits not dissimilar to what you would find people wearing at a carnival in Rio. I briefly wonder how they manage to move in them, let alone dance so freely.

I am just about to tell Luke I need the toilet when a cute redhead comes over and plonks herself on his lap. She throws me a territorial look and within seconds they start snogging. Feeling decidedly relieved and not in the least bit jealous, I hop off the seat in search of Shawna.

The club is bigger than I thought, and I end up circling it a few times before spotting Shawna in a dark corner sitting astride Pierre. She is laughing hysterically at something he has just said. Half a second later they are kissing. I roll my eyes, take a long drink of my beer, and watch the throng of dancers from my spot at the edge of the dance floor.

"Can I get you another?" a deep voice says from behind me, making me jump.

"Shit," I say, spilling half the beer down my top. I turn around and look up into a pair of familiar green eyes. "You," we both say simultaneously.

"What are you doing here?" I ask, the tone of my voice sharper than I intended.

He looks me up and down, his eyes lingering on my chest. "Pink Floyd, eh? I hadn't pinned you for an alternative chick."

I am immediately offended by his assumption. The fact that he is wearing a tight fitted black shirt and expensive looking jeans, with his hair perfectly coiffed, is exactly what I expected from him. "Funny," I say, waving my hand up and down at him. "I had you sussed from the moment I met you. There's plenty of women here without any brain cells, so I guess this place is right up your alley." I ignore the look of surprise on his face and peer around his shoulder. Walking towards us are his brothers, Max and Bryce. Bryce grins when he spots me, showing a set of perfect white teeth, and Max looks at me with one eyebrow raised, a slow smile spreading across his face. "Well, if it isn't the Ice Queen," he says.

"Well, if it isn't the Three Brothers Dim," I quip, watching the smiles fall from their faces. I down the rest of my beer and slam the glass on the table next to me. "Night boys," I say, turning my backs on them. I can feel the heat of their gaze as I walk across the dance floor and up the stairs to get my coat. I don't give them a second thought as I head out of the club and back to the chalet.

A few slippery minutes later I am back inside. The place is as I left it, aside from a mug tipped upside down on the draining board. Funny, I'm pretty sure I put everything away after I'd made myself tea and toast earlier. Shrugging, I head to the lower ground floor past the long glass wall, on the other side of which is the pool, sauna and steam room, and head into my room. I peel off my clothes, and despite the freezing walk back, a light sheen of sweat is covering my legs. I remind myself never to wear those leather trousers again. As I undress, an errant thought enters my head. Feeling decidedly rebellious, I grab a towel from my en-suite, wrap it around my body and head out into the pool area.

The pool itself has underwater lighting which highlights the expensive-looking blue mosaic tiles, and the room is lit a soft pink, giving the space a very exclusive spa-like feel. I walk across to the loungers and drop my towel on top of one, enjoying the warmth from the underfloor heating and the thrill of being naked. For a moment, I allow myself to imagine that the chalet is my own home and try not to squeal in excitement at how ridiculously happy that makes me feel. The locals were right, this place *is* a palace. I step down into the pool. The water is like a warm bath and I sink under the surface gratefully. Once acclimatised, I begin swimming lengths, completely butt-naked. It is quite exhilarating. Up and down I go, concentrating on how the water feels against my skin. I've always been good at swimming and have been on my school swim team. At least I was until I had to pull out in my last year due to Mum becoming more of a problem. She would turn up at my club pissed and almost always caused a scene. I dropped out through sheer embarrassment.

After a good half hour of doing laps, I decide to test my underwater swimming skills. I manage to make it from one side of the pool to the other in one breath. When my head breaks the surface, I am startled to find myself staring up at Green-eyes.

"Well, hello again," he murmurs, his eyes roving over my nakedness. My body finally catches up with my brain, and I attempt to cover myself.

"As much as I appreciate a naked woman as well as any man, do you mind telling me what you are doing in our chalet?"

My mouth pops open as my brain struggles to find an answer. *Our chalet?* Eventually, realisation dawns. "You're my designated family?" I say, just as Max and Bryce step into the room. They stop talking as soon as they see me.

"Damn," they say in unison.

FIVE

"I can explain," I say, trying and failing to hide my naked body from the three men, who seem to be having way too much fun watching me squirm. In the end, I give up, figuring they've seen it all already. "Fuck it," I murmur under my breath. Deciding I'm likely going home anyway, I walk up the steps totally starkers and grab my towel, wrapping it around me.

All three men are looking at me with their mouths gaping open and I can't help but feel secretly pleased by their reaction. I'm not normally this confident, but for some reason their arrogance pisses me off. I have these men marked; they love women and I am a woman. In this situation, I feel that my sexuality is the only power I have. Somehow, I know that being coy will give them one over on me and for reasons completely unknown to me, I do not want to give them the satisfaction of making me squirm.

"Perhaps we misjudged you?" Max laughs. "Not so much the Ice Queen now."

"We didn't even have to chat you up or buy you a drink to

get your clothes off..." Bryce smirks as he swipes a hand through his shoulder length hair, which is now hanging loosely around his face. "Really, there's no need to leave on our account. We were just about to take a swim, weren't we, Hudson?"

I gape at Bryce. What a prick. If he thinks I am getting back in the pool with them, he's got another thing coming.

Hudson shakes his head as if coming out of a daze. He looks at me, his green eyes stormy.

"I think you should get some clothes on then meet us back upstairs in the kitchen. We should talk." With that, he turns to his brothers. "Upstairs, now," he says, and they file out behind him.

I take a deep shuddering breath. What the actual fuck did I just do? My high quickly comes crashing to the ground when I realise I've just stood completely starkers in front of them all. I groan. One word pops into my head. Sacked. My mum will have a field day and Richard... Oh, god, Richard is going to be so disappointed.

Resigned, I go back to my room, pull on my tracksuit, pile my hair up in a messy bun, pack my bag, then head upstairs to face the music.

"What have you got there?" Hudson asks as I walk into the kitchen. There is a pot of coffee percolating on the counter, with four mugs set out beside it. The three brothers are sitting around the kitchen island, apparently waiting for me.

"My suitcase. I'll arrange for a cab to take me to the airport. I'll just hang about there until I can get a flight back home," I say, all fight gone out of me now.

Bryce gets up and walks around the island towards me.

"Give me that," he says. "You're not going anywhere. There's heavy snowfall due. You wouldn't be able to get a cab now even if you wanted to." He places my bag back by the stairs, then sits back down on the stool. As he walks past I feel decidedly tiny against his tall frame.

"But, I thought…"

"Look. So you used the pool, big deal," Max says, shrugging. "Besides, it was quite entertaining," he adds, giving me a wink. Bryce punches him on the arm.

"Ow, what was that for?" he says, shoving his brother back.

"Pack it in you two," Hudson says, giving them both a glare. He turns to me. "You'd think that now they've reached the grand old age of twenty-five they'd be a bit more sensible. Alas, I think the sight of a hot, naked woman in our pool has sent them spiralling back to puberty again."

Hot, naked woman? I almost laugh out loud. Did he actually just say that?

"Seems like we're not the only one whose brain has been affected, or perhaps it's another part of your anatomy," Max says, laughing. Hudson ignores him and pulls out a stool.

"Come and join us… we still don't know what your name is, even though this is the third time we've met."

"Isn't that usual for you guys? I mean, get a woman naked first, ask names later, if at all?" I swear I have absolutely no clue what has come over me but, clearly, I'm determined to insult these men tonight.

Hudson's gaze is heated with anger. Still, neither he nor his brothers try to deny it. Only Max has the decency to look a little sheepish. When I look at Bryce, there is a challenge in his hazel eyes, and I am not sure I like it.

"Your name?" Hudson demands. This time the friendly tone is gone. I almost want to lie, but in the end, I figure it's pointless.

I take a seat at the island and lay my palms flat on the table. "My name's Louisa, Louisa Budd. I'm your designated chalet girl."

"Well, we totally lucked out," Max says, high-fiving Bryce. He holds his hand up to Hudson, who just rolls his eyes. "Ah, man, don't keep me hanging."

I can't help it, I laugh. Max is clearly the joker of the family. If he wasn't such an egotistical prick, I could get to like him.

Hudson pours four cups of coffee and hands out one to each of us. "I thought it would help, you know, sober you up," he says, nodding to the cup.

I frown. He clearly has no idea what being pissed looks like. "I don't need to sober up. I'm not drunk," I snap, taking a sip of the bitter tasting coffee. I crinkle my nose, then in a saccharine voice say, "Can I have some milk and sugar, please." I almost flutter my eyelashes at him, but don't. I'm pushing my luck already.

Hudson is staring at me as though trying to get a grip on how I tick. "Do you usually swim naked then?"

"Oh, yes. I'm well known for it down the local pool." I smile sweetly and pass him my mug. I don't know why I feel the urge to needle him but every time I've met him, I have this desire to put him in his place. Him and his cocky brothers.

36

He takes the mug from me with a shake of his head, confusion furrowing his brow. A moment later he gives it back. I take a sip and savour the sweetness. "Hmm, that's better," I say, licking my lips. Our eyes meet and there is a flash of desire in his. Although it is entertaining being admired, I feel no pull towards him. Instead, I feel inexplicably angry and I don't have the faintest idea why.

Max sniggers. "Fuck, I don't think I've ever seen Hudson lost for words. I think you and I are going to get along."

I turn to Max. His brown eyes are twinkling with mischief. He oozes a boyish charm that I am sure most women lap up, but not me. "So long as you don't try your chat up lines on me, we'll get along just fine."

Max laughs loudly. "It's a deal," he says, although there's something about the way he's looking at me that gives me the impression he's a man who doesn't keep his promises.

"So, you've decided to stay then?" Bryce says, brushing a hand over his beard. He twists some of the hair between his thumb and finger as his strange, multifaceted eyes rove over my face.

"I don't think so," Hudson says, glancing at me. He's angry now. "Louisa should go as soon as the snowstorm passes."

I narrow my eyes on him. I get it, he can't overpower me with his charm and good looks so now he's using my one mistake against me. I think about what I have to return home to: a drunken mum and Christmas in A&E. Well, to hell with that. I am staying whether he likes it or not. "Actually, I don't think I will go."

Hudson looks at me sharply. I can feel Bryce and Max's

hot stare, but I don't look at either of them, too busy staring Hudson down. "I'm pretty sure I can use the facilities, so long as the guests agree to it and it doesn't take away from my duties. I had no-one to ask so, technically, I've done nothing wrong. Now, if you'll excuse me, I've had a long day and I need to go to sleep." I slide off the chair and pick up my suitcase, throwing a look over my shoulder. "Breakfast will be ready at eight am sharp."

With that I head back to my room, hoping I've made the right decision, but something deep inside tells me I may be making the biggest mistake of my life.

SIX

I wake up at seven am, shower and dress in a pair of blue Levi jeans, a thermal long-sleeved top, and a loose grey sweatshirt. My hair is thoroughly tangled, and it takes me a good five minutes to brush a comb through it. Last night I only managed to get a few hours' sleep after lying in bed thinking about the way I had behaved. I'm pretty sure the brothers went out again at some point after I returned to my room; not that I care what they get up to, it's their holiday, after all. What bothers me now is how rude I was to the brothers. I am not normally so confrontational. When I think about it, I know it's because I am damaged goods. My mum and her trail of boyfriends have fucked me up so thoroughly that I am pretty much in self-defence mode all the time.

This morning I have some apologising to do, but first, a trip to the local store is required to get supplies. The shop is a ten-minute walk into the main resort and open from seven am. All the chalet girls use it, apparently. I figure if I go now I will be back in time to cook them breakfast. Perhaps we can start again. Fresh day, a fresh start and all that.

I head out into the hallway and catch one of the brothers swimming in the pool. The underwater lights aren't lit so all I can see clearly is the top half of the swimmer's body moving through darkened water. Whoever it is has a huge, black, dragon tattoo penned into the skin of their sculptured back. It's not Max as he's blonde and it isn't Bryce as his hair is longer, which only leaves Hudson. I watch as he reaches the edge of the pool, turns and spots me. For a moment, my breath catches in my throat at the long look he gives me. He just stares, and I stare back. I feel like a deer caught in the headlights, wanting to move but suddenly unable to. What the fuck is wrong with me? Am I really going to pieces over a half-dressed man I don't even like? I watch as he swipes a hand through his wet hair. He walks to the steps of the pool and climbs out, turning to face me. He is completely and utterly naked. My eyes widen just a fraction as I take in his broad shoulders, defined pecs, six pack, and strong, muscular arms, finally resting on his manhood. A small smile plays at the edge of his mouth as he looks at me looking at him. Despite my bravado yesterday I find my cheeks heating, and not wishing him to see how much he's affecting me, I look away.

Arsehole, he totally did that on purpose. I turn on my heel and head upstairs, my heart pounding treacherously in my chest.

The ground floor is quiet as I enter, just the sound of coffee percolating in the machine. Max and Bryce are likely still sleeping and, glad I don't have to make small talk, I pull on my ski jacket and winter boots. When I open the door, my mouth drops open at the amount of snow covering everything in sight. "Shit," I say, my breath coming out in warm puffs. A snow plough is making its way down the street, pushing huge piles of snow to the side. I've never seen anything like it.

I head outside, enjoying the muffled quiet that only heavy snowfall can bring, and walk towards the main strip where the supermarket is located. It takes me less than ten minutes to gather what I need. The check-out girl tots it all up and I hand her the company credit card I've been given to pay for the food with. I still can't quite believe there is a couple of grand stacked up on the card to use for supplies. When Shawna handed it over to me, she said she had 'borrowed' a couple hundred quid from the card and paid it back on payday, implying that I could 'borrow' some money too. It's just as well I am trustworthy. This job means more to me than a few hundred quid.

"Merci," the girl says, handing me back the card after ringing up the bill. I thank her and make my way out of the shop.

A minute later I am struggling back up the incline, trying to hold on to two full bags of shopping whilst trying not to break a leg.

"Hey, Louisa, let me help." I turn and almost fall on my arse, a particularly icy patch making my feet skid beneath me.

"Whoa," Max says, catching me in his arms. The breath of his laugh tickles my ear. "Steady, you could break something," he murmurs, a little too sexily for my liking. He props me upright, turning me to face him. I am still ensconced in his arms.

"Okay?" He looks at me, the dark of his eyes a liquid brown. The air has suddenly got decidedly warmer.

"I'm fine," I say, pulling away.

"Sure thing," he chuckles, swiping a hand through his dishevelled hair.

"Good night?" I ask, realisation dawning. The relaxed pull of his mouth, the softness of his features. Max is clearly in orgasm thrall.

"Pretty entertaining, as it goes. A night with me always is. You should try it," he adds, a slow smile pulling up his lips.

"I think I'll pass."

He falls into step beside me and I can feel the light touch of his hand on the base of my spine, as if he's ready to catch me should I fall again.

"I can't believe how much snow there is. I've never seen anything like it," I say, stepping away from his touch. His hand falls away and I catch a strange look in his eye, but he says nothing.

"This? This is nothing. You haven't seen anything yet. Wait until you get up the mountain. When the snow falls up there, well, it's incredible." Max's face lights up as he describes the view. I can't help but smile at his enthusiasm.

"Are you going to ski today? I could show you around."

I shake my head. "No, I haven't come for skiing."

"Oh," he says, taking one of the bags from me. "What have you come for, then?"

"I needed the money," I say. It is easier to say that than to tell him I'm running away from a drunk mother.

"I see," he says.

We reach the steps and head back inside the chalet. When I walk in there is a brunette woman dressed in a man's shirt sitting across Bryce's lap. She is gorgeous, with long limbs and full lips. She is also vaguely familiar. She smiles at Max, her expression changing as soon as it rests on me.

"You've got a *maid*. Great, I'm starving." *Maid*? Fucking cheek. Immediately my back is up at the look she gives me, as though I am a piece of shit on her shoe. Then I notice the sparkling outfit in the corner and I remember where I've seen her before.

"I see you got yourself a *pole dancer*," I say, looking her up and down. "How much did you pay her for a private lap dance, Bryce?"

I hear Max snigger beside me.

"You bitch…" she says, getting up.

Bryce stands, a look of horror on his face. "Candy, isn't it time you got dressed and went home?"

"Candy? My name is *Clara*," she storms, walking away from Bryce and down the hall.

"Candy, I mean Clara," Bryce calls after her. He catches my eye as if he's waiting for a reaction. What the fuck is going on? Are all the brothers trying to get a rise out of me this morning or is this normal behaviour? I wonder briefly whether Hudson has a woman in his room too, then shake the thought away, not willing to think about why that bothers me.

"Eggs and bacon alright for breakfast?" I ask Bryce as he gets up, avoiding the fact he is bare-chested and muscly as hell. He has those super sexy muscles that taper in a V-shape towards his groin, the kind most men would die for and most women want to lick. "Or do you prefer sausages with your eggs?"

Bryce shakes his head, muttering something I can't quite

hear under his breath as he rushes down the hall after Candy or Clara or whatever the hell the bitch is called.

Twenty minutes later Clara is gone, and Bryce, Max, and Hudson are all sitting around the kitchen island eating the breakfast I've cooked them up. For a split second, I feel a sense of peace watching them eat, but it is gone as quickly as it appeared.

"Pretty mean fry-up, Louisa, thanks," Max says, jumping up and pressing a quick kiss to my cheek. By the look on his face, I think he is as surprised by the sudden show of affection as I am.

"You're welcome," I say, waving him off. "It's no big deal." I almost raise my fingers to the spot where he kissed me, but I don't.

"Well, I'm hitting the slopes, you coming?" he says to his brothers.

Bryce nods his head. "Yep, I'm up for that. I'll meet you at the lift in twenty. I've just got to get ready first," he says, heading off to his room.

"Cool, bro, I'll catch you there in a sec. What about you, Hud?"

"Maybe later. I've got some stuff to do."

"Ah man, we're here to play, not work."

"All the same, there's something I've got to do," Hudson says as he glances my way.

"It's fine with me. I'll just wash these dishes then get out of your hair," I say.

"Well, catch you later, guys." Max pulls on a woollen hat and heads out of the door, leaving me alone with Hudson, who sits nursing his coffee. Not wishing to start a conversation with him after that weird stare out in the hallway this morning, I gather up the empty plates and start washing them at the sink. Outside the view is almost entirely white, interspersed with tiny spots of colour. I can already see a line of people dressed in bright ski wear as they trudge through the newly fallen snow. People are laughing, happy. Kids are running around throwing snowballs, giggling when they hit their target. I watch as a father leans down, picks up his daughter and spins her around in the air. A sudden sadness spreads through me at their happiness. That is what childhood should be filled with; laughter, fun, love.

"There's a dishwasher for that," Hudson says, breaking my reverie.

"I know. I don't mind washing them up. It gives me something to do," I say, dipping my hands into the warm, soapy water, concentrating on the task at hand. A sudden tension has filled the air and I am trying my best to ignore it.

I hear the scrape of the stool as Hudson gets up, but rather than leaving, I feel the sudden warmth of his body heat as he stands close behind me. My hands stop what they are doing as Hudson's muscular arm slides around the side of me. A breath catches in my throat as he eases the plate into the water. I stiffen as he remains pressed against me, his other hand slipping around my side, so I am trapped in his arms. I can feel the thump of his heartbeat through my back as he takes my soapy hands in his, rendering me totally immobile. Not certain whether I am incredibly offended by his assumption that I would welcome his touch, or incredibly turned on, I don't attempt to stop him. He is a total dick, but a goddamn sexy one. Flashes of his naked body appear in my mind and I look up at our reflection in the window opposite. He is staring at me unashamedly.

"Louisa," he breathes, dipping his head to press a hot kiss onto my neck. Then he pushes my body forward, so I'm pressed up against the sink, his chest, hips, lips all pressed up against me so there is no space between us. Trapped there in his arms, my heart a dozen race horses galloping in my chest, I do something that surprises me. I close my eyes and lean my head against his shoulder. An involuntary moan slips from my lips as Hudson runs the tip of his tongue over the curve of my ear. I can feel the pad of his thumb massaging the palm of my hand as his fingers slowly trail up my arm. The warmth of his touch is gone for a moment until I feel his still wet hand slide up the front of my sweatshirt and beneath my vest. He rests his hand against the curve of my stomach, his fingers spreading wide over my skin, his little finger dipping under the waistband of my jeans. The firm press of his hand and the gentle graze of his lips against my skin ignite something within me, something I've never felt before, something that scares me. I turn my head to the side so that our mouths are almost touching. Hudson's evergreen eyes are hooded with desire.

"I have wanted to touch you from the very first moment I saw you." His voice is hoarse, gravelly, and for one sweet moment, I want to touch him back.

"What the actual fuck?" I hear Bryce say from behind us.

Hudson steps away, wiping his hands on a tea-towel as if he'd just been helping with the dishes rather than trying to seduce me. He is calm, cool, *triumphant,* and I know in an instant that I have just been played. I pull my eyes away from him and look at Bryce. There is a heated look on his face and for some reason, I feel ashamed. I feel like my mother whoring herself out to the first man who shows her the least bit of interest.

"Fuck you," I say, tears pricking my eyes. Hudson starts to open his mouth, but I push past both him and Bryce, grab my coat and head out into the cold.

SEVEN

I take a walk to the bottom of the first piste and sit on a wooden bench, watching a group of kids, no more than five or six years old, move across the flat snow on tiny skis. Their ski instructor makes them follow him in a single line so that he looks like a mother duck and they are his ducklings. Then he stops and gets them to line up in a row in front of him. He looks in my direction and waves. I press my finger into my chest and he laughs, pulling his ski hat and goggles off. It's Pierre.

"Hey, Pierre," I call, waving back. I watch him as he looks down at all the kids and pulls a face. They all laugh like he's the funniest thing they've ever seen.

"He is so goddamn cute, isn't he?" I turn to see Shawna walk towards me, a huge grin plastered over her face. She sits down next to me on the bench. "So, what happened last night? You went downstairs with Luke, then when I tried to find you later you'd gone. When I asked around after you, some really fit guy with the greenest eyes and the sexiest smile I've ever seen said you'd left."

"Yeah, sorry about that. I was a bit knackered. Decided to head back early."

"Sure, no sweat. That fit guy though, he was *smoking hot*. He was with two other men. The bearded guy was all over one of the dancers. I heard he asked her back to his place after her shift had finished."

"He did. She left not long ago."

"What?" Shawna says, her mouth dropping open in a delighted laugh. She claps her mitten-covered hands together. "You mean your *family* are those three hotties. Did any of them come with a girlfriend?"

"Nope. I basically think they're here to fuck," I say, remembering Hudson's hand on my stomach.

"Ah, it all makes sense now," Shawna says, her face lighting up.

"What makes sense?"

"They are the brothers Freed."

"Freed? That's their surname?" I laugh at the ridiculousness of it. "I suppose they like to be *free* to get into women's knickers."

Shawna giggles, shuffling up next to me on the bench. "Apparently, they're not really brothers. That's just what they tell everyone. Rumour has it they all grew up in some care home and that all of them had shitty mothers."

My head snaps around to look at Shawna. "Who told you that?"

"Luke told me about them, or rather he warned me about the brothers Freed when I first started here."

"Is that so?"

"He said there were these three brothers who come

here every year for the whole skiing season. That they are wealthy, love to party, and *love* women. According to Luke, they shag their way through the holidaymakers, resort staff, chalet girls, locals. A different girl every night. They're a bunch of lotharios and are amazing in bed by all accounts, but emotionally fucked-up. Like, big time."

"Yep, I reckon that just about sums them up," I say, feeling angrier by the minute at Hudson's advances. What a total prick.

"Well, shit. If I were you I'd be offering myself up on a platter. They are ridiculously gorgeous." She looks at me and I can't help but laugh at the face she pulls, even though there's no way I am going there. Nope, the brothers Freed were off limits.

"I'm telling you, Louisa, there isn't a hot-blooded woman on this planet who wouldn't get her clothes off for one of those three hunks."

"Well, there's me," I say, trying to forget the moment by the sink with Hudson a few minutes ago. That had been a complete lapse in judgement.

"I don't believe it. You can't tell me you wouldn't jump in bed with one of them, given half the chance?"

"They love themselves a bit too much for my liking," I mumble.

Shawna narrows her eyes at me. "What aren't you saying? Please tell me you shagged one of them?"

"No, I haven't shagged one of them, and I don't intend to either. The brothers Freed are not for me. I don't do damaged goods," I say, mostly because my own damaged soul is enough to contend with. There isn't room in my life for any more.

"Hudson, how are you doing, mate?" a man says as he's skiing towards us. Shawna and I both flip our heads around and find ourselves staring at the brothers Freed. All three are looking at me. All of them look pissed as hell. *Fuck.*

For the rest of the day, I avoid going back to the chalet. I don't want another confrontation with the brothers, so I take a trip up the mountain instead to observe the skiers as they speed down the slope. Despite it being cold enough for snow, the sun still feels warm on my face, and I understand now why so many people have a tan. The view from the café is incredible. When I sit in the outside seating area I feel as though I am on the top of the world, and that all my troubles back home are just tiny specks of dust like the skiers at the bottom of the piste. But my feelings of freedom and peace are short lived when I realise I must go back to the chalet to prepare the evening meal and face the brothers once more. I pay for my drinks and food at the bar then take the lift back down the slope. Half an hour later I am back at the chalet.

"Well, if it isn't our very own Ice Queen," Max slurs as I enter.

The place is heaving, full of people I don't recognise and some that I do. Clara, the bitch from this morning, is draped around Bryce's shoulders, her cherry lips pulling on his earlobes. For some ridiculous reason, it pisses me off. Clara whispers something in his ear, and he turns to look at me, his eyes narrowing. When Clara kisses him, he pulls her close, all the while looking directly at me. My heart drums way too loudly in my chest and I turn away just as Max stumbles forward. This time I'm the one to catch him. He can barely stand up straight. I take the can of beer out of his hand and manoeuvre him through the throng of people.

"I think you should go lie down before you pass out," I say. He really must have knocked back a lot of booze, considering a well-stacked guy like him could be so thoroughly drunk. He is almost at the stage of oblivion. I recognise the signs, I've seen it often enough with my own mother. When I look around the room, most of the people are in no better state than he is. I guess this is the *partying* Freed brothers Luke had told Shawna so much about.

"I'll help you get him upstairs," Hudson says, approaching us. He places an empty glass on a side table nearby and wraps Max's arm around his shoulder. There is a woman watching us. She looks older, more sophisticated than most of the other revellers in the room, with long blonde hair a few shades darker than mine and the prettiest steel-grey eyes. She is stunning.

"Hudson, do you need me to help?" she asks.

He turns to her. "No, Louisa and I can manage. I won't be long, Sacha."

"He's had too much to drink," I say, stating the obvious. I can feel Sacha's eyes on me. She's taking the opportunity to look me up and down as though I am a threat. I give her a smile, one that says there's no need to worry about me, but she just raises a haughty eyebrow. I dislike her immediately.

Hudson nods his head. "Max tends to knock the drink back when he's hurting."

Hurting? Why would he be hurting? I don't ask, not sure I want to get into a conversation about some girl Max might be pining after.

Together we manage to get him upstairs and into his bedroom. I haven't been in it before now and I am surprised by the sheer size of it. In the centre of the room is a huge king-sized bed covered in soft cream blankets, complementing the warm wood of the walls. We lay Max down. Hudson takes his shoes off and pulls an eiderdown over him, and then he does something completely unexpected and extraordinarily tender. He leans down and kisses Max on the forehead. It's not at all sexual, more like a father kissing his son at bedtime, but it surprises me nonetheless. Hudson turns to face me and, noticing the look on my face, sighs.

"Despite what you might think, I'm not a complete arsehole. None of us are."

I don't say anything, we just stand and stare at each other. I can tell he has more to say, so I wait.

"The rumours you heard are true. We are not blood-related, although in every other way Max and Bryce are my brothers. I have looked out for them since we ended up in the same care home together. I left at eighteen, worked hard, got a place. As soon as they were old enough to leave a couple years later, we moved in together. We've been inseparable ever since. We work together, we still live together. I don't think that will ever change. We've achieved a lot in the past eleven years after leaving the care home."

I nod my head. "And the women? Sacha?" I say, waving

my hand around, hoping he understands what I mean. What I really want to know is why he set his sights on me this morning. Why it had been so important for him to make me want him. *Wait? Did I want him?* I shake the thought aside, not willing to go there. Besides, he's clearly moved on already. Or rather switched his sights to someone else.

"They are a symptom of a fucked-up issue we all have..." He sits on the edge of the bed, careful not to disturb the now sleeping Max, and looks up at me, his green eyes flecked with pain. "We were all abandoned by our mothers. Not all in the same way, but abandoned nonetheless. I guess we find comfort in the arms of women. Fuck, I don't know. Sacha is someone I've known for some years. We're fuck buddies, that's all." Hudson pulls a shaking hand through his hair. For whatever reason, he feels the need to share this information with me. I'm about to ask why when he gets up off the bed and walks towards me, standing just inside what is a comfortable distance. Remembering the way he made me feel earlier, I step back, needing space between us. A strange riot of emotions clamour for my attention but I push them down.

He looks at me wide-eyed. "Christ, I have no idea why I feel the need to share any of this with you. I don't know what it is but there's something about you, something I recognise..." His voice trails off at the look of horror on my face. Am I that emotionally scarred by my mother that everyone can spot the deadness inside me?

"What did I say?" Hudson raises his hand to my face as a rebellious tear falls from my eyes. I am stronger than this. For so many years I have kept this well of pain within me, and for some reason amongst these men it is trying to escape.

"You are not the only ones to have suffered a cruel childhood, Hudson. Although my mother is still in my life, she abandoned me a long time ago for the oblivion she could find at the bottom of a bottle. So, I get what it's like. I understand, truly."

Hudson moves towards me, surprise, guilt, then sorrow tracking across his features. I take another step away. "Perhaps Max is right, perhaps I am the Ice Queen. I don't have room in me for more lost souls, my own is more than enough to deal with. Besides, I wouldn't give away something so precious to a person who uses women so carelessly. I've seen my mother do that time and time again. That isn't me," I say, my voice cracking with emotion. I turn away from Hudson and walk towards the door.

"Louisa," he says, staring at me. He looks so lost, so vulnerable that I almost, *almost*, go back into the room.

"Yes?"

"I'm sorry, for earlier. That was the fucked-up me, the one that needs to make every woman he meets want him. You don't want me, or any of us it would seem, and it made me mad. I guess I wanted to prove to myself that I could have you if I wished. I was an arsehole. I didn't mean to upset you. I'll back off."

I look up at him, at the tiny beauty spot that sits just under his eye, at his full pink mouth. I look at Max sleeping peacefully on the bed, I remember the look in Bryce's eyes as I ignored his attempts at making me jealous this morning, and sigh.

"You're all beautiful, any woman would be mad not to be flattered by your advances. But I can't give you what you want. I'm too broken already to allow any more people in to break what's left of my heart. I can't just have sex without it meaning something. I won't be used like that, and none of you can have meaningful relationships. That's pretty clear."

"Louisa…" he starts, but I hold my hand up.

"Hudson, I am not like other women. I won't be a part of any games, yours or your brothers'. I'm going to go to my room now. Tomorrow, when Max has recovered and you guys are alone together, I would appreciate it if you can make clear to them both what my position is. I am here to work, that is it. There is nothing beyond that. Fuck whoever you want, just don't try to fuck *me* over. If you don't think you can do that, then I will happily swap with another chalet girl."

With that I turn on my heel and head to my room, passing a scowling Sacha on the way down. I don't care if she heard what I said, I am no threat to her. It's all the other available women she needs to watch out for.

EIGHT

S ince my discussion with Hudson two weeks ago when
Max passed out at their impromptu party, the
boundaries I have put in place have seemed to work for us all.
The brothers have stopped trying to get into my knickers and
we have settled into an easy, relaxed rhythm. Every morning
breakfast is dished up at eight am. We sit and chat together
whilst we all eat, then we spend the day apart. I hang out on
my own or with Shawna and the brothers go skiing, or
fucking, I'm not really sure what they do with their day, and
frankly, I don't ask. Then we come together again in the
evening for supper where we sit and discuss what we've done
in the day or talk about general, light-hearted stuff. The
conversations never get deep, the brothers never mention the
women they are seeing and somehow an easy friendship has
begun to form between the four of us.

This morning I am feeling revived after an early morning
swim in the pool and a quick go in the sauna. The brothers
have no issues with me using the facilities so long as

breakfast is served at eight am sharp. Turning back to the task at hand, I dish up the full English breakfast they have come to expect every morning and place the warmed plates on the kitchen island. My phone rings, making me almost drop a plate when I see who's calling.

"Hi, Mum," I say, trying to hide the note of dread in my voice. She hasn't rung me at all since I've been here. Had it not been for Richard's regular texts I wouldn't have known what was going on back home. Last night he sent me a message saying he thought Mum was up to something fishy and warning me that there was trouble brewing. Hence the nauseous feeling when answering the phone now.

"I need five hundred quid," Mum says. No hello, how are you? No, how are you getting on? Christmas Day is only three days away, but there's no mention of that either. Mum's straight to the point as always.

"I don't have five hundred quid, Mum," I say. "I don't get paid until the end of the month. Can't it wait until then?"

"No, it can't bloody well wait. I need the money now. I've got a loan shark after my arse. They'll get nasty if I don't find the money soon," Mum whines.

I have the sudden urge to scream. "Can't you ask Dom? Maybe he can help you out," I say instead.

Mum's laugh is high and brittle. "Dom's fucked off and Paul hasn't got that kind of money."

"Who's Paul?"

"My new fella of course," she says. "*Please*, Louisa. I wouldn't ask if I had the money myself."

Frankly, there is fat chance of Mum ever having any money. She doesn't work, and all her benefit money goes on booze. "All right, Mum. I'll get it for you," I say quietly, not wishing for the brothers to overhear my conversation. "But you have to give me a bit of time."

"I don't have time. It has to be today, or I'm screwed."

I almost say, 'aren't you always' but I hold my tongue, not wishing to get into an argument with her.

"Fine, I'll sort it," I say, clicking my phone off and chucking it onto the kitchen counter. I knew this would happen. I knew this was too good to be true. I've been here just two damn weeks and she's already asking me to get her out of some shit she's got herself into back home because I am not there to babysit her. How in the hell had she managed to get herself into trouble with a loan shark? "Damn it," I say, slamming my hand on the counter. Why can't she stay out of trouble? Why can't she leave me alone?

"Everything alright?"

I turn around to see Bryce staring at me. He's dressed in a soft black tracksuit slung low over his hips and a tight fitting white t-shirt. His hair is pulled up in a high bun on his head and his beard is neatly groomed, even though it's early in the morning.

"Fine," I say, giving him the best smile I can muster. "Chalet girl stuff, that's all."

He nods and sits on one of the stools.

"Morning, Icy," Max says as he skids into the room.

"Morning, Jester," I retort, laughing despite myself. He's such a big kid at heart that my nickname suits him perfectly. Besides, he calls me Icy, so I have to get my own back somehow.

A moment later Hudson steps into the kitchen with

dishevelled hair and sleep still pulling at his eyes. He isn't much of an early riser, but he always gets up with his brothers because, well, that's just what he does.

"Morning," he mumbles.

"Morning, Hudson," I say, handing him a cup of coffee.

"Shall I ask Louisa then?" Max says, looking from Hudson to Bryce.

"Ask me what?" I say, dishing up their breakfast.

"Well, if you haven't already noticed, it's Christmas day soon and Bryce, Hudson and I usually head out to a cabin further up the mountain. It gets a bit busy down here in the resort. We thought you might want to come too," Max says, almost shyly.

"I see." I glance at each brother in turn. "I'm not sure. I mean, I don't want to get in the way of your celebrations. I imagine you'll have company. I'll be fine on my own." I take a sip of my lukewarm coffee and peer at the brothers over the rim of the cup.

"There won't be anyone else. Just us, and you. If you want to join us that is," Hudson says, his eyes never leaving mine.

"But I thought you'd want to have, you know…" I wave my hand around in the air. "Company," I finish. Sex, that's what I want to say. Basically, it sounds like the perfect place to take a few girls and have an orgy.

"We've never invited a woman to the cabin, but we'd like *your* company. None of us are particularly interested in anyone else's right now," Hudson says, then slams his mouth shut. Bryce and Max both give him a look that makes me think there is more to this request than meets the eye.

"Um, I don't know."

All three of them are staring at me whilst I dither between my sudden desire to be alone with them in a cabin in the mountains, and the urge to run screaming from the chalet. I can see Bryce's expectant look, Max's hopeful expression, and Hudson's hot gaze and I feel incredibly uncomfortable in my skin all of a sudden.

"It'll just be a couple of quiet days hanging out and eating," Max says with a shrug. The strange thing is, although he is acting like it's not a big deal, I can tell he really wants me to say yes. There's almost a look of desperation about him. Bryce and Hudson are the same, they seem way too tense for this to be a casual request.

"Tell that to all the girls hankering after you three. I'm pretty sure most of the females in the resort would love to join you and would happily take my place," I say, trying to make light of what is fast becoming a very tense situation.

"Like Hud said, we don't *want* anyone else," Bryce says, his hazel eyes darkening so that they are almost the same colour as Max's.

"We thought it would be fun," Max chimes in, his voice slower, more sensual than usual.

Thank God there is a kitchen island between me and the brothers because right now I feel as though they are all about a second away from doing something stupid. My heart is beginning to thump erratically in my chest as my mouth opens and closes like some dumb-arse goldfish. I am saved from responding at all when my phone rings loudly. I snatch it up from the counter. It's Mum.

Flipping open the phone, I walk from the room listening

to my mother's tirade whilst the brothers Freed watch me walk away from them yet again.

NINE

L ater that evening I sit at the table with the brothers, swallowing down the rising sickness I feel and trying to act like nothing's the matter.

"You're not hungry, Louisa?" Hudson asks, pointing to my half-eaten lasagne.

I plop my fork on the plate, giving up on trying to eat. "Nope, I'm not feeling that great. I don't have an appetite tonight."

"Do you think you're coming down with something?" Bryce asks, a look of concern on his handsome face.

"Nope, just a cold or something. I feel a bit bunged up, shivery. I'll be fine with some paracetamol and an early night," I say, ending the conversation. They eat the rest of their meal and talk about their day on the slopes, every now and then giving me surreptitious looks. I pretend not to notice. As soon as they are all finished, Hudson gets up and starts clearing the table.

"Hey, you don't need to do that," I say, placing my hand

on his arm. His eyes flick up and I snatch my hand away, the skin of my palms burning from the contact.

"We want to," Bryce says, looking between me and Hudson. "It's about time we took care of you." He's doing that sexy thing with his voice again and it's distracting me. I look at Max helplessly, but he too has a strange look on his face like he's about to do something silly.

"Erm, thanks. I'm just going to sit on the sofa, watch a movie then. Have fun this evening."

"You shouldn't be alone if you're unwell. One of us will keep you company," Hudson says from his spot in the kitchen.

"Don't worry about it, honestly. I'll probably just turn in early." I go and sit on the sofa and start flicking through the choice of movies that are available to watch.

It doesn't take the three of them long to tidy up and after a few minutes they are making their way to their rooms. I can hear the low murmur of their chat, but I can't make out what they are saying. I imagine it will have to do with which one of them is willing to stay behind, not that I want any of them to do that. The fact that they are willing to spend their own precious holiday time staying in with me when they could be out having fun makes me feel so much worse.

A wave of nausea hits me as I recall the five hundred pounds I stole this morning. Trust me to have a mother who gets herself in trouble with a loan shark then uses her daughter as a cash cow. The hate I have for her right now is toxic, making the nauseous feeling worse. I've never stolen before, but Mum had sounded so scared, desperate even, that

I couldn't think of anything else to do. I'm not due my first wage packet until the end of the month, and no matter how much I hate my Mum for putting me in such a predicament, I can't allow anything to happen to her. So, I did what I promised myself I'd never do, I withdrew the money from the cash machine in the resort using the credit card I'd been given to buy supplies. Then I deposited the cash into my bank account and transferred it directly into Mum's account. It had been that easy.

Now, as I sit on the sofa absentmindedly flicking through the cable channels, I hate myself even more than I already do, and a very real pain blooms inside my chest.

"Here, take this," Max says, bringing me out of my worrisome thoughts. I push them aside as he strolls towards me. He's wearing a pair of slacks and a loose jumper. In his hand is a hot-water bottle. I guess he's drawn the short straw to stay behind with me.

"Thanks," I say softly, surprised by his consideration.

He settles himself next to me. "I've decided to stay in tonight, keep you company," he says, making himself comfortable. His blonde hair is rough dried, and he smells of the vanilla shampoo that has become so familiar now. I find myself having the sudden urge to lean in and sniff his hair. *Stop it. Don't even go there.*

"Good, you've got the hot water bottle. That should help with the chills." I turn my head and Hudson is staring at me, a strange look in his eyes.

"Where are you going tonight?" I ask, noticing the casual attire he is wearing.

"I'm not going out." He looks at me, his eyes trailing over my face.

I smile brightly, trying to hide my growing nerves but almost jump out of my skin as Hudson sits beside me. Stealing that money has sure made me a nervous wreck. I really hope the brothers don't notice and start questioning me about it.

"You don't have to, Hudson. Max has already said he's staying in. I'm sure Sacha would be glad to see you."

Hudson frowns. "Sacha and I are history."

"Why?"

"I like someone else," he says, shrugging.

"Oh," I say, not sure why that makes me feel worse.

"Actually, we're all staying in," Bryce says as he strolls into the room. He too has showered and changed into something more comfortable than skiwear. He has a pair of soft slacks on and a fine-knit, grey jumper.

"Are you okay with that?" He chooses to sit on the floor rather than the sofa, and I can feel the warmth of his arm as it presses against my leg.

"Sure, okay," I murmur, not certain that I am okay, given the strange mix of nausea and butterflies I'm feeling.

"What are we watching then?" Max asks, gently prising the control from my hands.

"You choose," I say, feeling decidedly antsy in close proximity to all three brothers. Granted, I've been alone with each of them separately these last couple weeks, but the air seems charged differently tonight and I'm not sure what to make of it. Probably a mixture of guilt from stealing that money and the strange looks the guys keep giving me.

Bryce presses a button on another control, which dims the lights and closes the curtains automatically, whilst Max picks a movie. I don't pay much attention to his choice, acutely aware that both Hudson and Max have somehow moved in closer to me. Bryce is resting his hand on the floor so close to my foot that I can feel the warmth of his finger as it brushes against my skin. That touch alone has my heart hammering in my chest. It's so loud, I am certain they can hear it.

About halfway through the thriller we are watching, a scene comes on where the main character is seducing a woman. The sex is graphic, and I find my heart rate increasing, not because of what I am watching, but because the atmosphere in the room has changed from charged to electric. I breathe in sharply when I feel Bryce's warm hand curling around my ankle. That sudden intake of breath seems to ignite something within the room.

"Damn it, Louisa," Hudson groans into my ear at the same time as Max presses a kiss against the side of my face. Stunned, I clutch onto the hot water bottle, pressing it into my belly.

"What are you doing," I whisper. It's a stupid question, it is pretty damn obvious what they are doing, but I need them to answer me.

"You must know how we feel about you," Hudson says, pressing his soft lips just behind my ear. A thousand traitorous tingles rush down my spine and pool in my belly at his words and his touch.

"I don't know what you mean…" My words are lost in the warmth of Hudson's mouth as he gently turns my face to him and pulls me in for a kiss. His kiss is slow and gentle, and sweet, and nothing like I expected. As Hudson's kiss deepens, as his tongue explores my mouth, I am acutely aware that Bryce has shifted position and is now kneeling between my parted legs, his hands massaging my calves. They are firm and strong as they knead my flesh. Hudson pulls his mouth away and presses his forehead against my own, breathing heavily. He leans back and as I turn away from him, he gently pushes aside my hair and kisses my neck again, sucking slightly on the skin there. My eyes flutter closed until I feel Bryce's hands rest on my knees. When I open them, I find myself staring into Bryce's hazel eyes. As he moves towards me, the dim golden glow of the table-lamp casts a soft warmth across his features, making him impossibly handsome. Something catches in my throat as his gaze flicks from my eyes to my mouth. In a sudden rush of decisiveness, he has his hands tangled in my hair and his tongue shamelessly probing my mouth. The feel of his coarse beard against my skin only seems to heighten the kiss. I let go of the hot-water bottle and wrap my hands around his back.

Just at the point I find that I am losing myself entirely to the kiss, Bryce pulls away.

"I've wanted to taste that damn smart mouth of yours ever since you first talked back. For someone full of ice, your kiss is like fire, Louisa." He smiles at me then, letting out a small laugh to show me he means no harm by his words.

My hands fall away as he leans back down and begins massaging my legs again. I can't help but notice the bulge in his slacks and a small voice of warning pulls at my consciousness. A voice that is telling me this is what these men do, that I am no different from any other girl who has

70

melted under their touch. But I am distracted again by the featherlight touch of Max's fingers as they trail over the side of my breast. I turn to face him, and can see the desire in his eyes as he slants his mouth over mine. He pulls at my bottom lip with his teeth, the tips of his finger now grazing over my hardened nipple. Somewhere in the back of my head, a quiet voice gets louder. I am making out with three men, three men who had promised not to make a pass at me. Three men who I am beginning to grow fond of and who are now ruining our blossoming friendship with their need to fuck.

"I can't..." I say into his mouth, the little voice in my head stronger now. "Stop!" I push away at Max and his eyes open in surprise. I stare at Bryce, anger mixing with an overwhelming sadness that boils inside my chest. "Stop," I say again. He immediately drops his hands away. He too looks at me with a mixture of horror and confusion.

"Louisa, we didn't mean..." Hudson starts, but I turn on him. Holding my hand upright, I ignore the pain in his green eyes.

"Don't say another fucking word," I shout. I don't know why I'm so angry, I *had* been enjoying it, I had *wanted* them to touch me and yet, I am angry at them for going back on their word, for treating me like all the rest.

They're using you. They've planned this all along. You're no different from all the other women they've fucked. You're nothing but a piece of meat to them. They just want you for sex, for what they can get out of you. Just like those countless number of men who have used your mum.

I stand up, tears pricking at my eyes. "You promised you

71

wouldn't. I am not like all the rest... I am not like my mother," I whisper.

"Louisa, it isn't like..." Hudson starts. But I can't look at him, I can't look at any of them. Instead, I run from the room, angry tears pouring down my face.

TEN

The next morning, I wake up groggy and irritable but mostly sad. I've spent most of the night going over and over what happened, and I am alternating from being extremely pissed off, to acutely turned on, to incredibly, desperately sad. Most women my age would have jumped at the chance for such an encounter with the Freed brothers. A night of carnal pleasure. God, I have no doubt that it would have been pleasurable. It's just I don't want to be used like that. I won't be used and discarded like my mother has been countless times. Besides, they promised not to touch me, to respect my wishes, and they've broken that promise, just like Mum has done time and time again when she assures me she'll stop drinking.

There's a sharp knock at the door. "Louisa, I need to speak with you."

It's Hudson. His voice sounds pinched, guarded, but I don't care. He has no right to sound pissed off, none at all. I get up and pull the door open, wrapping my arms around my chest.

"Can I come in?"

"If I said no, you would do it anyway, so what's the point?"

Hudson swipes a hand through his hair, narrowing his eyes at me. Today they look more blue than green, like a tempestuous sea. There are dark circles under his eyes too and I feel a sense of satisfaction knowing he hasn't slept well either.

"Well, what is it?" I snap. Defence is the best form of offence. I'd learnt that particular trick many years ago.

"I see the Ice Queen is back on form again." His voice is stiff, cold.

"Whatever."

"I've just had a call from the resort manager, Bastian. He asked us how you were getting on. We ended up having quite an interesting conversation, actually."

"Oh?" I say, shifting uncomfortably on my bed.

"Yes. Bastian explained there has been an unusual withdrawal of cash from the card that was given to you to buy supplies. He wanted to know whether we authorised it, given we are funding the credit."

"The money on the card belongs to you?" I ask, my palms clammy. Shawna had said that the company credited the cards, not the individual holidaymakers. *Oh God.*

"Yes, that money does indeed belong to me and my brothers, Louisa. Bastian may be the resort manager, but my brothers and I own it."

"Own what?" I say, feeling confused. What does he mean?

"Brothers Freed own the resort. We don't like being stolen from."

"You own the resort?" My eyes widen as my hands begin to tremble. It doesn't go unnoticed.

"Yes. What I want to know is *why* have you stolen from us?" Hudson settles next to me on the bed, watching me carefully, but he doesn't try to fill the gaping silence that has descended.

I drop my head in my hands. "I'm sorry."

"So, you did take the money, then? Why, Louisa?"

"To give to my mother. She's in trouble with a loan shark. She needed the money. I didn't have any other choice," I whisper. I feel completely and utterly defeated. Hudson has every right to have me sacked, or worse, have me arrested for theft.

"We can come to an arrangement," he says, laying a gentle hand on my knee.

My head snaps up, and through the haze of my tears, I can see Hudson staring at me. "What kind of arrangement?" I say carefully.

"You come to the cabin with us today for Christmas and we forget about the money you stole."

"What?!" I say, pulling my leg out from under his hand, cool air replacing the warmth of his touch. I stand, backing away from him. "You want me to come to the cabin today on Christmas Eve like some hooker, so you and your brothers can have your way with me over five hundred pounds? Is that all you think I am worth?" *Five hundred measly pounds*? I'm pretty sure my mother gets more than that for her 'favours', as she likes to call them.

"No, that is *not* what I or my brothers think you are worth. This isn't coming out the way I planned..." Hudson stalks towards me, and I find myself caught up between him and the wall. "What I meant was, we're willing to ignore the theft if you are willing to spend Christmas with us in the cabin. We have no expectations of you, apart from your company and friendship. I promise you, Louisa, that's all we want."

I remember the previous evening and laugh almost hysterically. "That wasn't the impression I got last night."

"Last night got out of hand. It won't happen again," he says, taking another step closer to me. He's got that look on his face, the one that makes me think he is going to devour me any moment now.

"Where have I heard that before?" I laugh. Even now, even when he is trying to convince me that neither he nor his brothers will touch me again, he is still moving towards me as though he's going to do just the opposite. And the most fucked-up thing of all is that a large part of me wants his touch, wants to be adored by Max and Bryce too, even after everything I've said.

"And what happens if I say no?"

Hudson sighs. "Then we will arrange for flights to get you back home."

The air suddenly leaves my chest and I go lightheaded at the thought of having to return home. What would I be going home to? A pissed mother, her endless trail of dirty old men, and a mess I want nothing to do with but have got drawn into nonetheless. Looking at Hudson now, thinking about last night and the growing feelings I have for the brothers, just

76

makes me even more confused. I've stolen from them, I've been rude, defensive, jealous of the women they've been with, attracted to *all three of them* and yet done nothing but push them away time and again. Self-preservation is a fucking messed up bitch.

"Will you contact the police?" I say. I hate the fact that my voice sounds so small, weak. I hate that Hudson is the one who is making me feel that way, but most of all I despise my mum for putting me in this position at all.

"That depends on your answer, Louisa."

Tiny black spots start to speckle my vision at the thought that I could get into trouble with the police. It is mortifying enough I have stolen from them, but to be charged with theft on top of that as well. A stint in prison is not what I want to see in my future.

"Louisa, are you okay?" Hudson asks, concern creasing his brow. He reaches out, but I flinch away from his touch.

"Don't," I say, resigned now. "I will go with you, not because I want to, but because I can't bear to go home, and because I don't want to go to prison," I add, moving into the middle of the room and crossing my arms defensively. I hear the spite in my voice and cringe internally. Even when saying the words, I know I am not being entirely honest with myself.

"Then you'll need to pack. We're leaving in half an hour," Hudson says, his voice clipped, on edge.

"Half an hour?" I step out of his way as he walks past me. He stops at the door, turns around and considers me for a moment. "Yes, Bryce and Max have been out this morning and got everything we need for a few days away. Believe it or not, we are able to put together a pretty good

Christmas dinner," he says, attempting to lighten the conversation.

I narrow my eyes on him. "I don't care about your skills as chefs. I won't be eating it anyway."

"Fine," he snaps. "Just be ready in ten minutes."

ELEVEN

T he atmosphere in the car is as frosty as the layer of snow covering the winding mountain road. Bryce is driving, Max up front with him. Hudson is sitting on the back seat next to me. I haven't said a word since leaving the chalet, despite both Max and Bryce trying to make friendly conversation. I don't care. I am upset and angry and I feel betrayed. I thought we were friends. Stupidly, I had begun to believe that they cared about me, that they didn't just see me as a piece of flesh, but as a person. Then last night they caught me in a vulnerable state and tried to seduce me and now, this morning, Hudson has blackmailed me into going with them on this stupid bloody trip.

"Not much longer, the cabin is about ten minutes away," Max says, turning to face me. I don't bother to answer him, I just keep my eyes fixed on the view. Below, I can see the resort that the brothers Freed own getting smaller and smaller, the peaks of the chalet roofs and hotel disappearing the higher we climb. I still can't quite believe they own the damn resort. I mean, the information kind of jars with the fact they were all brought up in a care home. That sounds really shitty of me, I know. Why can't three boys from a care home grow up to be successful businessmen? In my experience, a shitty upbringing usually means a shitty life. In a different state of mind, I am sure I would have found the view beautiful and thought very differently. As it is, I feel a cold, empty, hollow space inside where my heart should be.

A couple more miles up the road, Bryce takes a left turn. The snow is deeper on the side road, but not deep enough that the 4x4 can't manage to traverse it without too much trouble. We pull up outside a small, single-story wooden cabin that has a wraparound porch. It sits nestled in the crook of the mountainside. Over to the left of the cabin is a forest of evergreen trees that fall away and down the side of the mountain. There are piles of logs stacked up on the porch and icicles hanging from the corner of the roof. Bryce jumps out of the car and opens the door for me.

"Here we are. Welcome to Petite Cabane," he grins.

"Thanks," I mumble, following Bryce across the crunching snow and inside the cabin whilst Hudson and Max fetch our luggage and supplies from the trunk.

Inside, the cabin is a smaller version of the chalet back in the resort. It has the same layout with a kitchen on one side and a small living room on the other, but instead of a flight of stairs separating the space, there is a single door. I assume that just beyond are the bedrooms and bathroom. It is a cute space, homely, cosy even, with red throws and pillows that match the kettle, toaster, and utensils hanging from little hooks in the kitchen.

"There are two bedrooms through the door. Take the one on the left. Hudson, Max and I will share the other room."

"There are only two bedrooms? I'll sleep on the couch," I say quickly.

"Absolutely not," Hudson says as he enters the cabin, a large box in his hands. "You'll take the room Bryce suggested."

"But…" I start to protest.

"No buts, do as you're told, Louisa," Hudson insists, giving me a look.

"Fine, have it your way. I'll just go unpack," I say ungratefully. I take my overnight bag from Max who has just entered the cabin and head through the door off the kitchen. On the other side, there is a corridor with two bedrooms facing each other. The one on the left has a huge king-sized bed that's big enough for several adults to have a small orgy, on the other a similar-sized room with a normal-sized double and a single bed in the corner. I wonder which of the brothers will share the bed and who is going to get the single. At the end of the corridor is the bathroom. When I push open the door I am surprised to find a large room with a pretty impressive jacuzzi bath in one corner and a large walk-in shower in the other. In the centre, between the two, is a sauna. Closing the bathroom door, I go back to my room and put away the few items of clothing I've brought with me into the large wooden wardrobes, then sit on the bed, wondering what to do next.

"Louisa, do you have a minute?"

I turn my head to see Hudson standing in my doorway. He

has his hands pushed into the pockets of his jeans and a strange expression on his face.

"Fine," I sigh, not really in the mood but knowing I'm going to have to listen whether I want to or not.

Hudson walks in the room and shuts the door behind him. He leans against the door and closes his eyes for a moment before swiping a hand through his hair.

"Why don't Bryce and Max know about the money I stole?" I ask him before he can make up some story I don't want to hear. I know he hasn't told them, Bryce and Max are acting like I wanted to come and wasn't bribed into coming.

"Because I didn't tell them."

"Well that's obvious, but why didn't you tell them?"

Hudson pinches his nose and gives a heavy sigh. "They wouldn't have agreed to me using that piece of information to get you here."

"I see."

"I don't think you do. From the moment you walked out on us last night, I knew you wouldn't have come along, no matter what any of us said. I did the only thing I could think of to get you to agree to come here…"

"So, you decided to blackmail me?"

"No," he starts. "I mean, it might seem like that, but I would never have sent you home or called the police." Hudson pushes off the door and comes to sit by me on the bed. He doesn't try to touch me or sit so close that he invades my personal space and I am glad of it.

"This isn't normal behaviour for me, Louisa. I swear to you, I am not normally such an arsehole." He looks at me and I raise my eyebrows. "Okay," he says, holding his hands up.

"You think I'm a womaniser, I am. You think I treat women badly, perhaps I do in the long run. But in the moment, when I make love to a woman, she is all that exists in the world. I am not a selfish lover, Louisa. Neither are my brothers. We worship women. Last night we would have worshipped you too." My heart does a flip-flop in my chest at his words and I curse myself, yet again, for being so damn mixed up when it comes to these men.

"What about respecting a woman? What about friendship, love? What about those things, Hudson?"

"Those are like the holy fucking grail for me. For Bryce and Max too," Hudson says.

"Sex isn't everything," I whisper.

"But it's all I know. At least it was until..."

"Until what?"

"Until I met you. Until *we* met you." Hudson takes in a shuddering breath and I have the sudden urge to reach across to him, to pull him into my arms. But I don't. I still don't know whether this is all a game, another ruse to get me into bed. Isn't this what he does, what they all do?

"How do I know this is not one of your tricks?"

"It's not. I know you may find that hard to believe after what you've heard about us, what you've seen, experienced. But this is me being honest. Completely and utterly honest. You've got under my skin. I know Max and Bryce feel the same. They were gutted to have upset you last night."

"All three of you? But there's only one of me, do you always share?" I laugh, and even though I'm pretending to be relaxed about it, my stomach is full of butterflies that I don't want to acknowledge.

"Never, but we'd be willing to share you if you're willing to have us. We wanted you to come here to Petite Cabane, so that we could just be with each other without distraction, without everything else getting in the way. Does that make sense? This is alien to us too."

I can see the raw emotion on his face. I consider Hudson's words. If this is all an act, then he's a damn fine actor. "It's hard for me to trust people, Hudson. I've been let down over and over again."

"I can see that," he says. "Perhaps that's why we're all drawn to you, we understand what it feels like."

"Truly, I am sorry about the money. I feel sick every time I think about it."

"I don't care about the money." Hudson presses his finger and thumb against his eyes. "I never did. I would have given that money to you in a heartbeat. I was a prick for using it as an excuse to get you here."

I consider Hudson for a moment. "I can't promise anything to you, Max or Bryce. For now, all I have is friendship."

"We'll take whatever you can give," he says.

TWELVE

We spend the evening cooking together, laughing and talking about our interests. For the first time in a while I feel happy. Hudson has lost his guilty look, Max and Bryce seem completely at ease in my company.

"So, you're telling me that last year Bryce went off piste and managed to ski himself into a tree?" I laugh so hard at the story my eyes are streaming.

"Yep, he had to hold a bag of cold peas against his groin for a week. It's a wonder his manhood still works," Max says, slapping Bryce on the back.

"Don't listen to Max, he's exaggerating. I'll have you know that my crown jewels are in perfect working order, thank you very much." Bryce glances at me and for the briefest of moments there is a flash of flirtation there, but he hides it quickly.

"Well, who's up for a walk outside? I need to burn some calories, I feel like the side of a house," I joke. Hudson really had surprised me with a beautiful dinner of marinated lamb, honey roasted vegetables and smooth, creamy, mashed potatoes. I am completely stuffed.

"Side of a house?" Max laughs. "Do you not know how incredibly sexy you are?"

I feel my cheeks burn at the compliment. I've never considered myself sexy. For the most part, I feel awkward in my body, choosing to cover it up rather than flaunt it.

"Max." Hudson's voice has a note of warning.

"I'm just telling the truth," Max says to his brother. He turns to me. "Sorry, Louisa. I didn't mean to make you uncomfortable. I'm not hitting on you, I'm just stating a fact. You are sexy. Sexy as hell. Whoever manages to capture your heart will be one lucky man." He smiles at me, a genuine, heart-warming smile.

"Thanks," I say, flapping my hand in an attempt to dissolve the sudden tension. "Walk, anyone?"

"We'll all come," Bryce says, grabbing his coat and hat.

Five minutes later we're all wrapped up in hats, gloves, and scarves and are trudging through the snow. It's deeper up here on the mountainside and is trickier to walk in but it is so worth the effort. I follow Hudson to the edge of the forest. Snow has begun to fall in thick, heavy flakes and all I can hear is the steady breathing of the three men standing next to me. The silence is as captivating as the snow and I breathe in the cold air as a gentle peace settles within me. "It's so beautiful," I say, completely enamoured with the place. "Is Petite Cabane yours too?"

"Yes, we bought the cabin and the surrounding five acres a couple years back after we fell in love with it. Even though we enjoy the chalet and the resort, this is our sanctuary."

"What do you guys do exactly?" I ask, curious as to how three relatively young guys have become so successful.

"We're into property," Bryce explains. "Hud worked his arse off after leaving the children's home. He had five jobs at one point. Then once we got out we worked our arses off too. It wasn't long before we managed to buy a studio flat. We did it up, we sold it on for a profit."

"Yep, then we kept buying, doing the places up and selling them on. We made a business out of it," Max continues. "Hudson here is the brains, Bryce and me the brawn." Max smiles and does an impression of the World's Strongest Man. I laugh.

"We owe all our success to Hud," Bryce says. I am caught by the love in his eyes. These men may have trouble committing to women, but they sure as hell are committed to each other.

"This business works because we *all* make it work, it's as simple as that really. Somehow, together we are better at a*ll* things," Hudson says, and I'm reminded of what happened last night. My cheeks flush at the thought. All three men are looking at me and I can't help but think they are reminded of last night too.

"Right," I say, clapping my hands together in an attempt to divert their attention. "It's beautiful, but it's damn cold. Who wants to go back in for a Baileys hot chocolate?"

"I wouldn't say no," Bryce says, and we make our way back to the cabin. Halfway through the walk back, Max stops.

When I turn around to see what he is doing I can see him rolling up a snowball. He puts his fingers over his mouth then throws it directly at Bryce, hitting him square on the back. I let out a delighted laugh at the look of mischief on Max's face.

"Oh no, you just didn't," Bryce says, scooping up a handful of snow and chucking it back at Max. It smashes against his chest, sending a spray of snow up in his face. Max's eyes widen as another snowball comes hurtling towards him, this time from Hudson, who is grinning wickedly. Before long we are all throwing snowballs at each other, running through the snow like a bunch of kids until we are laughing and wet from the fight. Ten minutes later I hold my hands up in defeat, giggling. Having lost my hat in the fun, my hair is a wet, snowy mess and even though I have a heavy jacket and jumper on, the snow has somehow worked its way under my clothes and I am beginning to feel cold.

"That's it, boys, I'm done. Time for that hot chocolate, yes?" I say, my teeth chattering.

"Sure thing," Hudson says.

"Just what I need," Bryce agrees, then swears as Max hurles one last snowball that hits him square on the jaw, covering his beard in snow.

"You look like Father Christmas," I laugh, and the brothers laugh with me.

Inside we take off our jackets, boots, and gloves and I head into the kitchen to start the hot chocolate. Max comes over as I am fetching the items I need from the cupboard.

"Here, let me do that. You look freezing, your lips are going blue," he says, his eyes firmly fixed on my mouth.

"I'm not *that* cold. Don't exaggerate," I say.

"Seriously. Go take a shower, you shouldn't sit around with wet hair and clothes, especially since you said you weren't feeling well yesterday. We'll call you when it's ready," Hudson says, pointing to the patches of wet on my clothes from where the snow has melted.

"Well, if you insist." I smile, grateful for their concern. "I was going to melt the chocolate, add milk, cream, and Baileys. Do you think you can manage that?" I ask, nodding to the items.

"Leave it with us, Ice Queen," Max says, saluting me.

I laugh. "Thanks, Jester."

Leaving Hudson and Max squabbling over the best way to melt chocolate, I head into the bathroom and strip off my clothes. The shower is surprisingly powerful and deliciously hot, and I spend a good five minutes just enjoying the feeling of the spray massaging my body, before rinsing off the remaining soap suds and stepping out of the shower. I grab a fluffy towel from the rack and wrap it around myself, almost jumping out of my skin when I see Bryce standing at the door watching me.

"Shit, sorry, Louisa," he says, turning away, but not before taking a good look at my naked body. "I knocked but got no answer. I just wanted to tell you the hot chocolate is ready," he rambles, a rather cute shade of pink rushing up his cheeks.

"It's fine, it's not as if you haven't seen me naked before," I laugh, trying to lighten the growing tension.

"Don't remind me," he grinds out. My eyes snap up to his face, to his hand that is gripping the door frame so hard his knuckles are white. Our eyes lock, and for a moment I am taken aback by the hunger I see there.

"I'll tell them you're coming." Bryce rips his eyes away and closes the door gently, allowing me the privacy to let out a shaky breath.

"Don't go there, Louisa," I say to myself sternly, even though my mind is thinking all sorts of dangerous things.

When I head back into the front room dressed in a soft grey jumper and matching slacks, my hair still damp from the shower, I find the brothers sitting on the L-shaped couch in the living room. Bryce looks up at me briefly before becoming very interested in the hot chocolate he is drinking. Max and Hudson smile.

"Come sit," Max says, patting the empty space between him and his brother. I look at the spot, then remember what happened last night.

"I'll sit by the fire. It'll dry my hair quicker," I say. Best to stay well away from close contact. I don't want another repeat of last night, do I? I shake my head at the wayward thought. "Is that mine?" I ask, pointing to a mug of delicious smelling hot chocolate on the coffee table.

"Sure is, darling," Bryce says. *Darling?*

Choosing to ignore the term of endearment, I swallow a mouthful of the delicious tasting hot chocolate, loving the taste of Baileys as it hits the back of my throat.

"What's the plan for tomorrow? Is there anything you'd like me to help prepare for Christmas dinner? Can you believe it is actually Christmas tomorrow?" I realise I am rambling, but can't seem to help myself. The atmosphere has got decidedly tense all of a sudden.

Max looks at me, his dark brown eyes like hot coals trailing over my face. "There's nothing you need to do. We've got it covered," he says.

"Okay." I find myself turning away from three sets of hungry eyes and stare into the fire. Memories of last night come unbidden into my head and I feel a rush of heat pool between my legs. I know these kinds of thoughts are dangerous, I had made it plain to Hudson not more than a couple hours ago that friendship is all I can offer, and yet here I am thinking about the way they make me feel. The way all *three* of them make me feel. Pushing those thoughts away, I concentrate instead on drinking the hot chocolate and running a hand through my still wet hair. I didn't bother giving it a thorough comb through when I got out of the shower, so it's pretty tangled as my fingers get caught up in the knots.

"Here, let me brush it for you," Max says, walking into the room with a brush in his hand. I hadn't noticed he had got up, too distracted by thoughts of last night. I go to protest, but he just smiles sweetly.

"It's no big deal Louisa, I just want to brush your hair. Can I?" he asks. There's a vulnerability in his request and I find I can't deny him.

"Sure," I mumble. What harm can it do?

He settles himself behind me, locking me between his thighs, and starts brushing my hair, taking extra care with the sections that are knotted. Before long I feel myself relax into his hold. He is exceedingly gentle.

"I used to brush my mother's hair before she got really sick. It's one of my lasting memories of her, and the only one that isn't filled with hurt and pain," Max says softly as he places the brush on the coffee table and begins to gently run his hands through my hair.

"How did she get sick?" I ask, glancing at Hudson and Max, both of whom seem mesmerised by what Max is saying.

"Mum was a manic depressive, they call it Bipolar disorder these days. Most of the time she was just plain sad, when she wasn't in a paranoid rage or hallucinating. The only time she seemed at peace was when I brushed her hair. Then one day she just flipped. She couldn't take her life anymore, even for me. She hung herself..." Max's voice trails off and I feel a rising sadness overwhelm me. When I look at Bryce and Hudson, I can see their own constrained emotions just beneath the surface. I place my mug on the coffee table and turn on my knees to face Max. He looks at me as though he is on the edge of a precipice and I am his only anchor keeping him from falling. "Max, I'm so sorry," I say, before pulling him into a gentle hug. He doesn't say a word, he just holds me with his face buried in my hair. We remain like that for quite some time until eventually he pulls away and smiles shakily at me.

"Well, Ice Queen, you sure know how to melt a guy's heart," he says.

I smile at him and give him a light kiss on his cheek before standing. "I think I might go to bed, if that's okay with you guys?" I say, all too aware that something out of the ordinary is happening between us. I know myself well enough to know that one more minute with them would mean all sorts of trouble for me. It has been a long and emotional day. Sleep is what I need. Well, that's what I tell myself anyway.

THIRTEEN

"Wake up, it's Christmas morning, you lazy oafs."

I smile at the sound of Max ribbing his brothers on the other side of the corridor and their grumbles of protest. Yawning, I sit up in bed and stretch. Outside the snowfall is so heavy I can't even see the forest. I think this must be what they call a white-out. The fact that I am inside, warm and cosy, whilst the snow is piling up outside makes me feel strangely happy.

I'm only wearing my underwear, so I pull on my fluffy dressing gown and socks before opening the door. Max is standing on the other side wearing a Santa hat. He immediately pulls me into a hug and presses a kiss on the top of my head.

"Happy Christmas, beautiful," he says.

I don't bother to pull him up on the flirting, it's Christmas day after all. Besides, I kind of like the way he looked at me when he said it. Like he meant I was beautiful, the *me* inside, not the way I looked on the outside.

"Happy Christmas, Max," I say.

Max is suddenly a big kid, full of happiness and energy as he pulls me along the corridor and into the living room. I have no idea why he's so excited, it's not as if there will be any presents. I stop short when I see a tree covered in fairy lights, twinkling in the corner of the room. Underneath are several presents wrapped up in brown paper and red ribbon.

"Wow, did Santa stop by last night while I was sleeping?"

"He may have done. Looks like Santa left a shed load of snow too," Max smiles, pointing to the window. "It doesn't look like we'll be going anywhere until this heavy snowfall has passed and the snowplough can clear the mountain roads. Luckily we have enough supplies to feed the five thousand."

"Thank goodness for that," I laugh, feeling excited rather than worried about the thought of being ensconced in the cabin with the brothers Freed. I don't know what happened overnight, but this morning I feel entirely different about the whole situation. "Well, all I can say is, Santa did a sterling job this Christmas."

Hudson and Bryce pile into the room looking exceedingly cute with their messed-up hair and sleep-filled eyes. For the first time, Bryce hasn't bothered to make himself presentable for breakfast and I can't help but smile at how adorable he looks.

"Santa had a bit of help," Bryce laughs, pulling his long hair up into a quick bun. "Merry Christmas, Louisa." He steps over to me and pulls me into a hug. This time I don't flinch or pull away, I just let him hold me. I barely reach his shoulder, so when I rest my head against his broad chest all I can hear is the steady rhythm of his heart beating.

"Happy Christmas, Bryce," I reply, stepping out of his hold.

"Right, let's get breakfast started. Pancakes, maple syrup and bacon coming right up," Max says.

"I'll give you a hand, bro." Bryce pecks me briefly on the cheek, then grabs a frying pan and drizzles oil into it whilst Max starts making pancake mixture. I watch them work together, laughing and joking. This is the first Christmas I have ever experienced without some kind of shit going down. All my previous memories of this day are filled with a drunk mother screaming and hollering, and a cold lonely dinner. When I see the brothers so full of happiness, a feeling of contentment settles inside my chest. It's refreshing, and I hang on to it wholeheartedly.

"You okay there, Louisa?" It's Hudson, he's perched on the back of the sofa watching me watching his brothers.

"Yes, I'm great actually," I say. It's the truth. Today, I am just going to enjoy being amongst these men. I won't let doubt or fear or worry about whether they are being genuine dampen my thoughts. I decide then and there that for one goddamn day I will allow myself this happiness and to hell with everything else.

"The Christmas tree, the presents," I say, pointing to them. "Did you do this last night after I went to bed?"

"Yes, we had the presents brought up yesterday and stored in the outhouse before we arrived. Last night we had the tree and decorations delivered. Max organised it and all three of us decorated the tree."

"You did?" I laugh. Hudson smiles too.

"Why is that so hard to believe?"

"Well, it's just so *perfect*." I look at the jewelled baubles on the tree, at the carefully placed ornaments. It is beautiful.

"Believe it or not, we love Christmas. Not growing up in a loving home meant we were deprived of what most people take for granted. It has become a tradition for us to celebrate together. We decorate the tree, exchange gifts, and cook together. This is the first Christmas ever that we've wanted someone to join us. I'm glad you're here," Hudson says.

We look at each other for a long moment and I see the sincerity in his eyes.

"Louisa, come here," he says, holding open his arms.

Without thinking too much about what I'm doing, I walk into them. His arms are warm and solid as they wrap around me tightly. We are almost the same height, him sitting on the back of the sofa, me standing between his legs. He presses his cheek against mine. "I hope you'll forgive me someday for the way I've handled myself, Louisa. You're special, we don't want to lose you," he says softly.

I pull away from him, looking into the depths of his green eyes. My heart flutters at the hope, at the honesty I see in them. As we stare at each other, the background noise of Bryce and Max cooking breakfast falls away. I don't know whether it is the magic of Christmas morning, my sudden decision to allow myself one day of happiness, or something else entirely, but whatever it is I leave the Louisa of yesterday behind and press a soft kiss against Hudson's mouth.

The moment our lips touch a raging desire explodes between us and I am acutely aware of Hudson's hands as they grip my hips, pulling me closer towards him. Something inside me snaps, and I tangle my hands into Hudson's hair, kissing him back with the same fervour he is kissing me with.

"Holy shit, guys. Our backs are turned for one minute…"

I pull away from Hudson, breathing heavily, and turn to see Bryce and Max staring open-mouthed at us. In that moment, in the privacy of the secluded cabin, whilst the snow falls heavily outside and the Christmas tree sparkles like magic in the corner of the room, I open my arms to the Freed brothers and they walk straight in.

"Are you certain?" I hear Hudson ask.

"Yes," I say.

Hudson stands just as Bryce walks towards me and for a moment I am sandwiched between both men. I don't feel afraid, I don't feel anything other than a desire to be loved. Bryce steps forward and lowers his mouth over mine. The kiss takes my breath away as his tongue laps at my lips and twirls with my tongue. As he holds me against him, there is no doubt of his desire for me.

"Ice Queen," I hear Max whisper into my ear, as his body replaces Hudson behind me. Bryce pulls away as Max turns me around to face him. There is delight in his eyes and something else, something close to adoration.

"This is the best damn Christmas present I have ever had." With that, his lips crash against mine as we kiss like there is no tomorrow.

I can hear the heavy breaths of both Bryce and Hudson as they watch Max and I kiss each other. I want more, so much more. It's as though something has uncorked within me as a rush of heat, and lust, and desire burns inside my chest.

"The bedroom, now," Hudson growls, pulling me from

Max's arms and lifting me into his. I wrap my legs around his waist and bury my head into his neck. Over his shoulder, Bryce and Max are following. I don't allow myself a second to debate whether what I am doing is right. I've only ever slept with a couple of men and never more than one at a time. This is new territory for me, but somehow it feels right. These men, for whatever reason, want to make love to me and I am going to let them and damn the consequences. For one day I want to not think about the real world and the upset and sadness it has brought me. I want to remain cocooned in the arms of these men. I want to feel something other than the broken pieces of me.

Hudson kicks open the bedroom door and lays me gently down on the bed, placing a tender kiss on my mouth. He stands back, not waiting a second longer to pull off his top and pyjama bottoms, leaving just his tight boxer shorts on. He doesn't seem to care that his brothers have entered the room, and doesn't flinch when they strip down to their boxers too. All their eyes are on me and it is thrilling and naughty, and incredibly sexy. The fact that all three of them have bulging pants has me squirming on the bed, itching to touch them. I've never felt so sexy or adored before.

Hudson remains standing at the foot of the bed, watching me with barely restrained longing whilst Bryce and Max move next to me. Max leans over and pulls apart my dressing gown, gently trailing his fingers across my skin, pressing hot kisses in the places his fingers have just left, following heat with fire. I find myself moaning under his touch. Bryce takes my mouth again, this time he gently coaxes me with his kiss as his hand moves to my back and unhooks my lacy bra. I find myself being lifted up off the bed as Max removes my dressing gown and pulls off my bra before lowering me back down again, leaving me naked aside from my knickers. Then two hot mouths close over each of my nipples and I am lost to the sensation of their tongues lapping at my breasts.

In all that time, Hudson remains where he is. There is desire in his stare, but there is something more, something I can't quite understand. Is it pain? Fear? I'm not sure, but I feel like I am losing him to his thoughts and I don't want him to go.

"Hudson, come here," I say, repeating his words to me earlier. Max and Bryce move aside, still beside me but stroking my body with their hands instead of devouring me with their mouths.

We stare at each other until I realise what he's waiting for. "I *want* you," I whisper. A hot rush of heat pools between my thighs at the groan that slips from his mouth.

He scrapes his hand through his hair, his chest rising and falling in heavy breaths. "I want you, *we* want you too, but I didn't bring…" his voice trails off. I hear Bryce, then Max swear lightly under their breath as realisation dawns on them too. I can't help it, I laugh. In the heat of the moment, the small matter of protection has slipped all our minds. Despite my very real disappointment, I am secretly pleased they were telling the truth when they said I was the first woman they'd brought here.

I sit up so that my shoulders are touching both Max and Bryce's chest. "We should stop," I say. I don't want to stop, I don't want to break the spell between us, but there really isn't any other option.

"No way," Hudson replies, his voice a low growl. "This isn't about us, this is about you, Louisa. There are plenty of ways we can please you."

"Yes, *we* can wait, but *you* don't have to," Bryce says as he leans down and runs his tongue along the curve of my ear.

"These hands are skilled," Max jokes, waving his fingers at me, a lust-filled smile pulling at his lips.

"Then I guess we don't have to stop," I say huskily, looking between my beautiful men. *My?* That thought alone makes me feel both excited and scared all at the same time. Could they ever really be mine or will the magic of today be over sooner than I would like? I don't get time to think about it as Hudson crawls up the bed towards me. Bryce and Max have to pull back for a moment whilst he settles himself on top of me, crashing his mouth against my own. Our kiss is passionate, all-consuming, and as he rocks himself against me, the thin material of our underwear the only thing separating us, I push all doubt aside.

"You are so damn beautiful, Louisa. I cannot wait for the moment I get to bury myself inside you, until then this will have to do," Hudson says, pressing scorching kisses across my skin. He moves slowly downwards until his mouth is pressed against the material of my lace knickers. With one swift movement, he removes them and covers the heat of my sex with the moist warmth of his mouth. Bryce and Max return to my side, both of them worshipping me with their hands and their lips, and as each of these damaged, beautiful, sexy men worship my body I find myself falling into the abyss of their devotion.

FOURTEEN

"I think I should finally get breakfast ready," Max says, planting a tender kiss on my cheek and untangling himself from behind me. Bryce gives him room to get off the bed.

"Look after her, brothers," he says with a wink, before leaving the room.

I settle myself between the two men, my face pressed against Bryce's broad chest. Hudson is behind me, the whole length of his body firm against the back of mine. I let out a peaceful sigh, undeniably happy in the moment. I feel satiated, but there is still a shimmering desire lingering within me, one that is burning brighter by the second. We lay there, the three of us, legs and arms tangled around one another, my nakedness wrapped in their arms. Raising my hand to Bryce, I trace a finger over the dark hair of his chest. Of the three men, he has the most body hair and I find it undeniably sexy. He oozes masculinity in a raw, powerful way and before I know what I am doing I am curling my hands in his hair and pulling him down for another kiss. Behind me Hudson groans, his own desire still apparent and pressing into my lower back. From behind, I can feel his hand move between my legs and I part them, so he can slip a warm finger inside of me. As Bryce kisses me like the starving, Hudson brings me to a climax with his skilled fingers. It doesn't take me long to become a hot mess in their arms.

Bryce pulls me into his chest and feathers kisses into my hair. "You hungry now?" he laughs.

"Yes, I'm starving," I say, still feeling the afterglow of the most amazing orgasm I have ever experienced. The Freed brothers are indeed incredibly gifted in bed, and that had just been foreplay.

"Breakfast is served," Max says from his spot by the door.

"Let's go eat now before I change my mind and make you come again," Hudson murmurs into my hair. I let out a delighted giggle.

"Hey, looks like I missed out on all the fun." Max crosses his arms and pouts.

I slide off the bed and saunter over to him, aware that I have not only Max's but both Bryce and Hudson's complete attention. Pressing my body against him, I trail my hand through his golden hair. "You're next, Jester." I have no idea where this sexy, confident Louisa has come from but she's here and I like her.

Max groans and covers my mouth with his. He tastes of maple syrup.

"Come on, put Louisa down and let's go eat. Have you forgotten there are presents to open," Bryce says with a grin, as he pulls on his pyjama bottoms and then hands me my dressing gown.

After eating the delicious breakfast and washing it down with a cup of Earl Grey, we all go and sit beside the Christmas tree. I tuck my legs up under me on the sofa as I watch the brothers hand each other presents. Max rips each one open with the delight of a child, Bryce and Hudson open theirs carefully. It's so sweet to watch and incredibly heart-warming. Before long each of the men have a pile of presents stacked up next to them. Weirdly, I don't feel out of place, just happy to experience my first Christmas amongst a loving family.

Hudson leans over and pulls out a gift bag I hadn't noticed until now. It's the last gift under the tree and I wonder which brother it is for.

"This is for you, Louisa," he says with a shy smile.

"*Me?*" I say, taken aback. I look at each brother in turn and feel my heart squeeze inside my chest. It seems to be doing that a lot lately. "You didn't have to do that." More to the point, when had they gotten around to buying me gifts?

"Open it, Louisa," Max says, grabbing the bag from Hudson and plopping it in my lap.

"I... thank you," I say, pressing a hand against the pounding beat of my heart. I can feel tears welling in my eyes. The last time I had been given a Christmas present was when Richard was still with Mum. Before he arrived, and after he left, we didn't do gifts. We didn't do Christmas, full stop. "You don't know how much this means," I say softly.

"Open it, darling," Bryce says. I catch his eye and smile.

Placing my hands into the gift bag I pull out something soft wrapped in red tissue paper. I unravel it and lift up a white Pink Floyd logo t-shirt, similar to the one I have.

"Look at the back," Hudson says.

I turn over the t-shirt and printed on the reverse is a slightly altered verse from the song 'Butterfly'.

"I don't know what to say." I look at Hudson, Bryce and Max, and my eyes fill with hopeful tears. If I'm honest, it isn't my favourite Pink Floyd song, but the words they picked out have to mean something, don't they? I re-read the last line again and again, my thoughts running wild with the possibility of what that could mean.

"There's more," Max says, gently removing the t-shirt from my grip.

I pull out a medium-sized box about the height of a book and gently prise open the lid. Inside is a beautiful figurine of a blonde woman dressed in a white dress, snow at her feet. In her hand, she is holding three hearts made of ice. I turn her over carefully, admiring the detail and craftsmanship. Whether it is coincidence or not, she looks very much like me.

"Our very own Ice Queen," Max murmurs. I look at him, at the hope in his eyes, and I am left speechless. Max takes the figurine from my hands and places it gently on the table. "There should be one more present left inside."

At the bottom of the gift bag is a black velvet box. I pull it out gently, my heart hammering loudly in my chest.

"Open it," Bryce says, a gentle smile curving his lips.

I flip the lid open, to find a delicate white-gold bracelet embedded with a row of sparkling diamonds. Nestled in the centre is a butterfly made out of blue topaz. My mouth pops open and I find that all capable speech has left me. I just sit staring at the beauty of it.

"You should wear it," Bryce says, getting up from his spot on the floor. He sits down next to me, takes the bracelet from the box and gently pulls at the edge of the butterfly's wing so it unclips. The bracelet opens, and he slides it onto my wrist.

"Beautiful," he says.

"Thank you," I murmur. "No-one has ever given me such thoughtful gifts." A tear slips from my eye as Bryce pulls me into his arms, pressing a kiss against my head.

"You deserve them."

"You deserve so much more," Max says, from behind. He gets up and I feel his arms wrap around me.

"And we want to give it to you," Hudson says, kneeling at my feet. He moves closer and wraps his arms around me so that I am held between them all. In that moment I realise one simple fact: I am falling for the Freed brothers, falling hard.

FIFTEEN

"As much as I like the thought of you naked under that dressing gown, it's rather distracting when we have a Christmas dinner to cook," Bryce laughs. We've been sitting and chatting about our interests and hobbies for the past couple of hours or so and it's nearing noon. I am surprised to discover that Bryce likes to paint and has a studio for his artwork back home in London. Max is a keen musician, and Hudson a writer in his spare time. So, not only are they handsome, skilled lovers and great businessmen, they are also creative and thoughtful. The combination is a complete turn-on.

"I'll go change, I don't want to distract you. I'm looking forward to this dinner!"

Leaving them to prepare, I head back to my room, taking my gifts with me. Not one of them has mentioned the fact that I have no present to give in return, even though I feel really terrible about it. Honestly though, up until yesterday afternoon, I still believed they were all lotharios that I should avoid like the plague. Buying them gifts hadn't been in the forefront of my mind. Now my opinion of them has gone full circle and I am pretty much in over my head. I know it's possible the growing feelings I have for them may change the minute we head back to the resort and reality sets in, but for now, in the magic of Petite Cabane, they are *all mine.*

Feeling utterly content, I pull on a pair of blue skinny jeans and a brushed cotton shirt over my underwear, then comb out my hair. Taking a look at myself in the mirror I decide to apply a bit of makeup and grab my toiletry bag from the side table in my room. I unzip the section where I keep my eyeshadow and laugh out loud at what I pull out. In my hand is a strip of condoms, three to be precise.

"Shawna." I grin at the gift she has given me. I vaguely remember her looking through my makeup bag that first night I arrived in the resort. I haven't worn makeup since that night and hadn't looked in the bag until now. Thank goodness for Shawna and her filthy mind. With a plan forming, I wrap each condom in a piece of the tissue paper left over from my gifts, slip the packages into my jeans pocket and head back out to the living room.

Bryce and Max are preparing vegetables and Hudson is covering the turkey in strips of juicy bacon when I walk back in. They are still half-dressed in their sleepwear, but all of them have an apron on. It is quite a sight.

"That's it. In it goes," Max says, sliding the turkey into the oven. "I'll pop the vegetables and potatoes on later."

"Quite the chef, aren't we?" I smile.

"Well, you learn to grow up pretty quick when you've

lived most of your life in care," Bryce replies. He's not being snarky, just honest.

"Sure, I totally get that."

Bryce pulls off the apron he's wearing and hangs it up on a hook. His bare chest is glistening slightly with a sheen of perspiration and I am reminded of the way his skin tasted under my lips.

"I'm going to take a shower. I won't be long," he says.

"Wait a minute, I have something for you. For all of you," I say. Both Max and Hudson look at me with a frown, but Bryce's lips curl into a smile. It's as though he can read me like a book.

"Is that so?" he says.

"Uh huh."

Taking off their aprons too, Max and Hudson sit on the sofa whilst I perch on the coffee table. My heart is thundering in my chest as I pull out the small packages and hand one to each of the men. Then, taking a deep shaky breath, I speak. "I have no idea what is happening between us all. I don't know if this is real or not, or just some fantasy we are all caught up in. All I know is that right here, in this moment, I want each and every one of you. I am willing to give myself to you all. I only ask that you don't use that unless you mean to give me a piece of yourself in return." I point to the gifts in their laps.

Bryce is the first to open the tissue paper. When he sees what's inside, he lets out a low whistle. He is careful not to show his brothers what's enclosed, he just looks at me like any minute he is going to pounce, and I had better be prepared for it. He nods his head.

"You can have any part of me, darling," he says.

I turn to Max, who is sitting opposite me, and watch him as he rips open the tissue paper. His eyes snap up as soon as he sees the silver foil packet.

"Damn it, Ice Queen, you've already stolen my heart. You can take the rest of me, I give it to you willingly," he laughs, a sexy smile breaking across his face.

Finally, I turn to Hudson, who out of the three brothers is the most reserved. He unravels the tissue paper slowly, then gently places my gift in his hand. I can feel the ragged thread of my pulse pounding in my chest as he raises his eyes to me.

"This is no fantasy, Louisa," he says, curling his hands around the condom and kneeling in front of me. He reaches up and gently presses the palm of his hand against the side of my face. I lean into his touch.

"Then what are you waiting for?" I whisper.

Hudson reaches up and pulls me into his lap, covering me with hot kisses. He kisses my lips, my cheeks, my nose. His teeth pull on the lobe of my ear. A moment later the coffee table is gone, moved away by Bryce and Max. Hudson lays me down gently on the soft sheepskin rug and unbuttons my jeans.

"Tell us what you want. We don't wish to overwhelm you, Louisa," Hudson says, as Max and Bryce kneel down beside me.

"I want you *all*," I whisper, holding my arms up to Max.

"Then that's what you shall get, darling," Bryce murmurs, the gold flecks in his eyes ablaze with fire.

Hudson leans over me and presses a gentle kiss against the bare skin above my waistband, then slides my jeans off just as Max leans in and takes my mouth with his. Warm hands unbutton my shirt, pushing the material aside as gentle fingers slide up under my bra, playing with the buds of my arousal. I am lost to their hands and their mouths as Hudson reaches into my drenched knickers and gently pushes his finger inside me, coaxing my body to relax further, to open up. I move my mouth away from Max and pull Bryce towards me, groaning at the different taste of his mouth, at the hungry way he kisses me.

The sound of foil being torn open has me breaking away from Bryce's lips and I watch as Max rolls the condom over the length of his cock. Lust, desire, perhaps even love, bubbles in my chest as Bryce and Hudson move away, allowing Max full access to me. Max leans over and places a tender kiss against my lips, then slowly peels my knickers off.

"Ice Queen," Max murmurs, a small smile playing on his lips. The way he says my nickname so tenderly makes me melt further.

"Not for much longer," I whisper back. He smiles and without a moment's hesitation leans over, shielding me from the others. I am lost to him as he pushes inside of me, lost to the way his blonde hair tickles the skin of my face as he moves above me, to the steady surety of his touch, to the flush of his pink lips as he kisses me and to the curve of his smile as he whispers my name. The feeling of him filling me with his length, sliding in and out of the warmth of my core, soon has me calling his name until we both come undone.

"Damn it, Ice Queen," he says. Max cups my face in his hand and presses a careful kiss against my mouth, removing himself gently. Then he pulls me into his arms and holds me, saying nothing until a feeling of peace and contentment blankets me.

"That was beautiful," Max says eventually. "I would stay here for the rest of my days if I could, but you want us all and I want you to have that. Bryce and Hud will take care of you now." Max gently removes my arms and gets up. I watch him leave the room, the flush of our lovemaking still very evident on our skin.

"Darling, come here," I hear Bryce say. He is sitting on the sofa naked, watching me with heavy lidded eyes. Hudson is sitting opposite, his green eyes raking over my flushed skin.

"Take your top off," Bryce says.

I stand, pulling my arms from my shirt, and unhook my bra, allowing my heavy, aching breasts to fall free of their constraints. Naked, my long hair falling around my shoulders, I approach Bryce. Hudson sucks in a shuddering breath as he watches me straddle Bryce's lap then lower myself slowly over the velvety smoothness of his cock. Tipping my head forward, I gasp at the delicious feel of him stretching me. He runs his hands over my back from the base of my neck to the base of my spine and back again, allowing me a moment to take him fully. Our eyes lock and in an instant, I am on my back on the sofa, Bryce pounding into me. He lets out an unbridled cry as I take him, all of him, my nails digging into the skin of his back. Bryce doesn't hold back, he is passionate and raw and virile and everything I hoped he would be. Trembling, he calls out my name repeatedly, the desperate need in his voice sending me crashing into a vortex of sensation as my body tightens around him.

"Darling," he utters, his body shaking from the aftermath of his orgasm. Bryce kisses me deeply, claiming me with his mouth until my lips are bruised and my breath is ragged. Then he pulls free and lifts me in his strong arms, lays me gently in Hudson's lap and walks away, leaving me alone with him. I am aching with want, on the cusp of losing myself entirely and I know it will take very little to send me over the edge once again. Max and Bryce have marked me as theirs and now it is time for Hudson to mark me as his.

"Best 'til last?" I ask, biting my lip. I am joking, of course, Bryce and Max mean as much to me as Hudson, yet I am nervous in his arms. He has this vulnerability about him, something that lurks just beneath the surface and I am drawn to it, to the broken parts of him. They call to me like a siren's song and I find myself wanting to drown in them.

Hudson smiles. "I am glad that I am the one who has the honour of taking you last. Are you ready, Louisa?" he says, brushing his lips against mine softly.

"Yes," I whisper back.

Hudson lays me against the sofa and kisses me slowly. He doesn't touch me or move above me, he simply savours the taste of me. For long minutes that's all he does, teasing me with his mouth, rendering me a writhing, hot, mess beneath him. Then he ever so slowly traces the tip of his tongue over the hard points of my nipples, teasing me with the lightest of touches. I go to grab his head, needing to pull his mouth over me, but he pins my arms to my sides as he continues to lick lower. His tongue swirls over my belly before his mouth rests over my sex. I try to buck against him, on the edge of losing my mind but he lets go of my arms and holds my hips steady, teasing and lapping against my swollen flesh until I can barely take any more. Then just as I am about to come, he pulls his mouth away and breathes warm air against me. The sensation has me squirming beneath him.

"Hudson, please," I whimper, a single, solitary tear leaking from my eye.

He pushes upwards, grabs the condom from by his side and rips the foil open, sheathing himself. I can feel the tip of his cock teasing my opening and I press my eyes shut, unable to contain myself as he lowers his body over mine.

"Open your eyes, Louisa. I want to look at you when you come," Hudson says, as he pushes into me with slow, smooth, control. His lips graze mine as he slides in and out of me. He doesn't rush, he takes his time moving with deep, even strokes, drawing me closer to the edge then bringing me back until I can barely stand it. Not once does he remove his eyes from mine, the sea-green colour of them like the calm before a storm. I can't help myself, I sob as a rising rush of warmth, starting in my core, blooms outwards, overwhelming me with the intoxicating power of it as the most exquisite orgasm rips through us both.

Once we have both come down to Earth from our sexual high, Hudson picks me up in his arms and walks me back to the bedroom, laying me down on the bed. My body is liquified in the afterglow of the brothers' devotion and I feel utterly relaxed.

Hudson cups my face in his hands, then brushes a soft

kiss against my forehead. "Sleep, Louisa, and when you awake, we'll be waiting for you. All of us."

I look up at Bryce and Max who have entered the room and something close to bliss settles over me as they both kiss me gently too. I have no idea what the future holds but right now, within the walls of Petite Cabane, I'm happy to suspend reality and lose myself to the avalanche of their desire.

SIXTEEN

A few hours later, I find myself curled around something warm and solid. My chest is pressed up against a firm back, my arm pulled around a smooth chest. We are both entirely naked. Beyond the closed door I can hear the sound of laughter in the kitchen and the smell of Christmas dinner being served up a few hours later than anticipated. I open my eyes to find myself looking at Hudson's beautiful dragon tattoo, which spreads across the entire span of his back. It's the first time I've really been able to study it. Apart from the startling green eyes of the dragon, the tattoo is drawn with black ink. It is so beautifully done, so intricate, it could almost be real. I look into the eyes of the dragon, at the strength, the determination, and I know that I am looking right at a piece of Hudson's soul. Whoever the artist is, they have certainly managed to capture the essence of Hudson in that image. I press my lips against the centre of his back, just on top of the dragon's head, then gently try to remove my arm.

"What do you think you're doing?" Hudson's sleepy

voice responds. He catches my hand, entwining his fingers with mine.

I smile into the crook of his neck. "I thought you were still sleeping, I didn't want to wake you."

He turns around to face me. Sleep has messed up his hair and crumpled his face a little, but he is still gorgeous, more so, for a little of the barrier he once seemed to have has fallen away. My heart does a silly flip-flop as he smiles lazily at me, the green of his eyes twinkling with mischief.

"You can always wake me up like this, Louisa," he says, lifting his hand to move away a fallen strand of hair that has slipped across my cheek.

Between us I feel the stirrings of his desire grow once again. I bite my lip, remembering how it felt to have him inside me, remembering how it felt to be adored by them, these men who are chipping at the ice surrounding my heart. I still can't quite believe I actually slept with them all. I barely have sex, let alone three men in one afternoon.

"How long have we been asleep?" I ask, suddenly feeling the need to change the subject. Images of my mother and her whoring herself out begin to blacken my thoughts. I am not like her, this is different. It feels right.

"A couple hours," he smiles, but it slips from his face when he sees that I don't return it. Urgh, why does my mum have to enter my thoughts now. Even when she isn't around, she manages to spoil everything.

"Louisa, what's wrong?"

"Nothing," I say quickly, trying to pull out of his arms, but he tightens his hold on me.

"Hey, don't do that," he says. "Tell me." He waits for me to speak, giving me a moment to gather my thoughts.

"I was thinking about my mum. The way she is with men. They use her, and she lets them. I don't want to be like that…" my voice trails off, unsure with how to continue.

"You think this is the same?" I can hear the hurt in his voice.

"No, no," I say quickly, realising how it must have sounded. "I just… All my life there has been a trail of deadbeat men who've used her for money, for sex, for a roof over their heads, for alcohol even. The only exception was Richard. He loved her, he tried to fix her. Richard was the closest I've ever had to a father. He's the one who got me this job. In fact, you probably know him, he's doing the marketing for the resort."

"Richard Shelby?"

"Yes, that's him."

"He's a nice guy, good at his job."

"Yes, he is. But they aren't all like Richard. Aside from him, Mum has pretty crap taste in men. Jesus, some of the people she's brought home over the years…"

"I'm sorry, Louisa. I'm sorry you had to grow up with that."

"Me too," I say, my voice cracking with emotion. Hudson pulls me tighter against his chest. It feels good to be held this way. An understanding, born of like meeting like, settles between us. "I'm not used to this…" My voice trails off as I have trouble trying to explain all the broken shards that are still embedded in my heart.

"Used to what?"

I can't say being loved, because I daren't hope for such a thing. Adored, perhaps; desired, most definitely. Earlier today, I felt both of those things. And yet, this is all beginning to feel more than that for me, much more. The brothers Freed have somehow broken down some of the barriers I've built to protect myself. That in itself is quite a feat and it scares the shit out of me.

"Feeling wanted, safe," I murmur, not quite able to watch his reaction. Rejection is something I'm used to, but it doesn't mean it hurts any less to receive it. My mum has rejected me every single day since I can remember, choosing oblivion over loving me. It was a lonely place growing up with a drunk, a dangerous one too, given all the seedy men she brought home. I push those thoughts aside, I don't want to go there. That place is too dark, those memories too painful.

Hudson doesn't answer right away, but I can feel his gaze fall over me. I wait for his rejection, because it's what I expect, what I've become used to.

"There isn't much I can promise, but for now having a safe place in my arms is one thing I can provide, Louisa," he says carefully. I know what he means. I understand what he isn't saying, that he is as broken as I am, that there are no guarantees that what we have found here in Petite Cabane will extend beyond these walls. Yet a small part of me remains hopeful, even though the larger, more cynical part is warning me to protect myself.

I bite on the inside of my cheek hard to stop the tears I know are threatening to fall. I am stronger than this. I have to live in the moment now, not think about tomorrow or the day after. It is the only way I've been able to survive. Don't expect anything and you'll never be disappointed.

"Thank you," I whisper. Hudson pulls me into his arms, wrapping them around me tightly so that I am pressed into his chest. He doesn't try to kiss me or turn this into something sexual and I'm glad. Right now, safety and comfort are what I need, what I crave. Sex is a by-product of that, a great one granted, but a by-product nonetheless.

He holds me close for a long moment until the door swings open and Max enters, a goofy smile spreads across his face when he sees us embracing. He takes a leap onto the bed, jumping on top of us both.

"Now what are you two up to, all cosy in here? Room for one more?" he asks, wiggling his eyebrows.

"Get off us, you great oaf," Hudson laughs, giving him a gentle shove as he sits up. Max tumbles rather dramatically over the side of the bed and falls to the floor. Hudson looks at me and rolls his eyes before flinging the covers back and stepping over his brother. I can't help but look at his tight arse and strong muscular legs. The dragon on his back ripples as he pulls on a t-shirt and jeans. He bends down, picks up a t-shirt, and hands it to me.

"Here, take this. I'm going to grab a coffee. Would you like one too?" Hudson asks as I pull it on.

"I'd love one, thanks." The smell of Bryce's aftershave tells me this t-shirt is his. I breathe it in, savouring the masculine smell.

"I'll make sure it's how you like it this time. Milk and two sugars, yes?"

"Please, I like it sweet."

"I know, I remember," he says, leaving the room.

Leaning over the side of the bed, I see Max lying on the floor feigning some kind of injury. I scoot over to the edge of the mattress and place my feet on the floor next to him, taking a step over his body. Max's hands shoot upwards, holding firmly onto my thighs so that I remain straddling him.

"Now this is a position I could happily stay in for quite some time," he says with a smirk.

"Ha, ha," I respond, trying to pull free, but he holds me firm. Perhaps it wasn't the best idea stepping over him with no underwear on. I twist my body around, and stare down at him, my hair falling forward.

He pulls himself up in a sitting position, sliding his hands higher up the backs of my thighs so that they rest just below the curve of my bottom. Bryce's t-shirt is more like a nightie on me, which is just as well given how close Max's face is to my sweet spot.

"I'm suddenly very hungry," he says with a dirty smile. "Can I taste you?"

Part of me wants to let him, the other part, the part that's used to shutting down all feelings, including the physical ones, seems to have taken over me and I tense under his touch. Sensing my change in mood the sexy grin slips from his face. He releases his hands, slides out from beneath my legs and stands.

"Hey, ignore me. You're just too damn hot. I feel like a hormonal teenager around you," he says with an easy smile, dissolving the sudden awkwardness and making me relax instantly. "Besides, Bryce will be pissed if I spoil my appetite, he's cooked up a feast for us all."

"Is that so?" I say, grinning.

"Come on, let's eat." Max drapes his arm around my shoulder.

"I should get changed…"

"Why? There's no need to get dressed up. It's just us."

"But I have no underwear on," I say, feeling a blush creep up my cheeks.

"All the more reason you should stay as you are." Max laughs at the look on my face. "Come on, Icy, let's go stuff our faces."

SEVENTEEN

After filling up on the most delicious Christmas dinner I've ever tasted, I decide a nice long shower is in order. Out of the window I can see that daylight is slipping away, even though it's only three o'clock. Nevertheless, Max and Hudson are keen to get outside and clear some snow, given the storm has lessened somewhat. Even though we aren't due back to the resort until tomorrow they want to get a head start on digging the car out. Even the thought that this little piece of paradise will be over so soon has my heart sinking a little. I don't want to go back to the resort, I'd much rather stay here forever with these men.

"I reckon we've had at least two feet of snowfall, if not more. It looks as though the worst of the storm has passed. The sky should clear some more overnight. Once the snow has been packed down, the pistes are going to be fantastic. I bet everyone in the resort is desperate to get back up on the mountain," Max says, staring out of the window.

"I imagine there are probably a few thrill seekers already risking their necks now," Bryce adds.

"I agree. If the roads are made passable tomorrow and we manage to get back to the chalet, I might join you on the slopes." Hudson smiles.

"You normally work Boxing Day," Max says, giving Hudson a surprised look.

"Not this year. This year I'm taking the day off. Perhaps even Louisa will be willing to have a lessen or two," Hudson says, turning to face me. He's pulled on his coat and hat, ready to shovel some snow from around the car.

"Oh, I'm not much of a skier," I say, shaking my head. Not much of a skier? I've never skied in my life.

"That's okay, we can help you get back on the horse, so to speak. It'll be fun," he persists.

"Fun?" Bryce laughs. "I don't think I've heard that word come out of Hudson's mouth for, well, ever. You've certainly done a number on Hud, given he's willing to give up a day of working for *fun*. I didn't think you had it in you."

"I can have fun," Hudson protests, feigning mock upset.

"Sure, your idea of fun is spending all day at work, then letting your hair down with several beautiful women beneath you," Bryce jibes.

"Bryce, man…" Max starts, noticing the look on my face.

I cover up my reaction with a false smile. "Hey, it's fine. You don't owe me anything, but I think I'll pass on the skiing," I say tightly, unable to hide the hurt I feel, even though I have no right to feel it.

"Damn it, Bryce." Hudson frowns at his brother. I catch his eye, and he starts to say something then stops. What can he say? Clearly, it wasn't a lie.

"Louisa…" Bryce calls after me as I leave the room. I try

not to feel hurt by the fact Hudson chooses, hell they all choose, to let loose that way. They have a history, these men, and a shed load of women and lots of sex are a huge part of it. I hate that knowing it makes me feel this way. Jealousy and doubt settle in my chest as I head into the bathroom and turn the shower on. Whilst I wait for the shower to warm up I grab my toothbrush, squeeze on some toothpaste and clean my teeth. Weirdly, one of my bad habits as a kid was to overclean my teeth whenever I felt upset or unhappy, which was often. It made me feel better, having clean teeth. I don't know why. I guess I associated bad things with shit teeth. My mum's were terrible, stained a dark yellowish brown from all the alcohol abuse and smoking fifty cigarettes a day.

I scrub and scrub them until I feel marginally better, spitting out the excess toothpaste and swilling my mouth with water once I'm done. I look at my reflection in the mirror, studying my face. "What are you playing at, Louisa?" I whisper to myself, then nearly jump out of my skin when I see Bryce staring at me from the doorway.

"I need to apologise for what I said," he starts, stepping into the room and shutting the door behind him.

"What, for telling the truth?" I say, turning around to face him.

Bryce sighs, scraping a hand over his beard. "No, for being such an insensitive prick."

I shrug my shoulders. "I'm not a child. You've all got a past, a reputation. I get it, you all like women, you've had a lot of them."

"Yes, maybe we have, but after what you said this morning, what you gave us..." Bryce blows out a frustrated breath. "Look, I'm not someone who's able to say how I feel without running for the hills. Give me a boardroom full of clients and I can go on forever about business stuff, but when it comes to stuff like this I don't know where to start." He walks over to me and I have to arch my neck slightly to look up at him. "I'm sorry if I made you feel like shit, it wasn't my intention."

"What about Hudson?"

"He's pissed at me and taking his anger out on the snow." Bryce pulls a face. "At this rate he'll clear a path all the way back down to the resort."

I sigh, feeling bad I've caused friction between the brothers, especially on Christmas day. It had been going so well up until that point. *Way to go, Louisa.* "I overreacted. Tell Hudson it's fine. Don't worry about it," I repeat, echoing my words from earlier. The knot in my stomach is still there, the doubt clinging to me stubbornly. "I'm going to take a shower, do you mind?"

He doesn't take the hint or if he does, he ignores it. Instead, Bryce steps closer to me so that I am backed up against the sink, my bottom pressing against the cold porcelain.

"You're not fine. What can I do to make you feel better?"

Love me? The rogue thought enters my head and for a moment I worry I've said it out loud. I consider what he's asking. I can't expect his love, nor can I expect it from Max or Hudson. Despite everything they've said, that's just a fantasy, unrealistic.

"I'm not sure there is anything that can fix me," I say. I

don't mean how I feel in this moment. I mean everything else.

"Your mum is pretty messed up, eh?"

"Yes. Messed up, broken, lost. She's all of those things, but she's still my mum…"

Bryce lifts my chin, his hazel eyes staring into mine. "She's lucky to have you and a fool for not appreciating what a beautiful person you are. I understand what it's like to feel rejected, worthless. I get it. I've felt it too, I still do." His voice tightens over the words and I wonder what his mother did to him to make him feel as unloved as me. A tear falls from my eye and rolls down my cheek. My ability, it seems, to keep my emotions in check is failing around these men. Bryce catches the lone tear with his finger, then leans close, rubbing the tip of his nose against mine.

"Tell me what you want, Louisa," he says against my mouth.

I wish I could, but I can't even begin to make sense of what I feel, let alone articulate that to him.

"It's why we do it…" Bryce starts filling the silence. He brushes his mouth against mine and I find my heart aching for more of his touch.

"Do what?"

"Have sex. When you don't know what it feels to be loved, you look for the next best thing."

"Like now?" I whisper, pressing my hand against his broad chest, holding him back.

"I want you. I can't deny that, I won't. After this morning, being with you is all I've thought about. Seeing you wearing my t-shirt, smelling me on you. I don't think I've ever wanted another woman more. All I want to do right now is lift you against this sink and bury myself in you, never coming up for air. You have bewitched me. You've bewitched us all." Bryce's chest is heaving, his arms are raised, trapping me within them. God, I want him too. I do.

"What do you want, Louisa?" he repeats.

I lean forward, pushing against his chest. He steps back, waiting. The tension is intense, it's difficult to breathe. I glance at the shower, then back at Bryce. Oh, what the hell. I let myself go earlier, I can do it again. Right now is for living, *feeling*. I will deal with the aftermath later.

"Take a shower with me?" I ask.

A grin spreads across Bryce's face. He leans down for a kiss, but I press my fingers against his lips. "But we can't..." I start, remembering we have no more protection.

Bryce pulls his t-shirt over his head and kicks off his slacks. "I'll behave, I promise."

His large hands fall to the bottom of my t-shirt, and as he grabs the material his knuckles slide upwards against my skin. The feeling sets off tiny sparks of fire inside of me. I moan out loud.

"If you make those kinds of noises I might not be able to control myself," Bryce says, his eyes darkening with desire.

He throws the t-shirt to the side and pulls me in for a kiss. I feel tiny against his large frame, he is my very own man-mountain and sexy as hell. Our mouths meet, yet this time his kiss is about as tender as I have ever felt. His hands slide through my hair, run over my back and cup my arse cheeks, squeezing them gently. Then he lifts me up and walks me to the shower.

The water is tantalisingly hot as it runs over our skin, and Bryce's kisses even more so. I can feel his cock pressing up against me. It is a dangerous position to be in, one slide downwards and all sorts of trouble will follow. I pull back, untangling my legs from his waist, common sense peeking through my lustfulness. Bryce eases me slowly to the ground, presses a gentle kiss against my forehead, then leans over and grabs some body wash. He pours some into his hands and rubs them together.

"May I?" he asks, waiting for my permission.

I watch the water fall over his luscious, rock hard body, watch as it slides downwards to where his cock stands to attention. I raise my gaze to his. "Only if I can wash you too," I say smoothly, surprising myself with my self-assuredness.

A low chuckle erupts. "Now that is an offer I can't refuse."

His soapy hands slide over my shoulders first, moving slowly down my arms, massaging in firm circles until they reach my hands. He presses his thumb into my palms then slides his hands back up. I take the opportunity to place my soapy hands over his chest, running my fingers through the coarse hair that I love so much before giving his nipples a gentle tug. His cock twitches at that, and I can't help but smile at the way his body reacts to my touch. My hands slowly move lower, sliding over the dips and grooves of his stomach muscles, until I hold his cock in my hands. It curves upwards, bold and virile.

"Louisa," Bryce says, sucking in a sharp breath. I look up at him, feeling suddenly powerful as I fist my fingers over his cock. I don't take my eyes off him as I move my hand up and down, my thumb swirling over the enlarged tip. He leans over, taking my mouth in his as water pours over us both. Bryce bites on my bottom lip, pushing me back up against the wall, his mouth moving over my face, my neck, sucking on my ear lobe. Low pants come from him as I work my hand quicker whilst the other cups his balls, teasing them gently. He is positioned in such a way that the firm spray of the shower hits the head of his cock. The combined sensation of my hand pumping and my fingers teasing has him slamming his hands against the tiles either side of my head as his body arches, his head tipping back. He calls my name over and over as an orgasm tears through him.

It takes a few moments for Bryce to come down from his high. When he does, he doesn't say a word, just presses a gentle kiss against my mouth, then he takes my shoulders and turns me around, so my back is facing him.

"Damn it, Louisa. I don't think I have ever come as hard. Now it's your turn," he whispers into my ear. Bryce begins to massage my shoulders and upper back, easing some of the tension that has gathered there.

"You have the most beautiful arse, like a ripe peach." He steps closer, his hands smoothing over my skin before sliding over my bottom. I can feel the coarse hair of his chest tickle against my back. I love the feel of it, of him pressed against me. His warm mouth glides against my neck as his hands trail down my arms. He lifts them up, guiding me to put the flat of my hands against the shower wall. I can feel the firm silk of his cock rest briefly against the crack of my arse before he stands back slightly with a groan. Bryce is still hard, despite his release.

"Louisa, what are you doing to me?" he says as his hands begin to massage my aching breasts. He pulls my nipples into hard points, twirling them gently between his thumb and fingers. Desire pools within my chest, blooming outwards. I am on fire.

"Bryce..." I moan.

He releases me from his teasing, sliding his hands over my rib cage and lower towards the heat of my sex. I am desperate for his touch, I ache for him, wanting nothing more than for him to press his fingers against my clit. Still he teases me as his hands move lower, smoothing the front of my thighs before circling around and cupping my arse.

"Spread your legs for me, darling," he says, kneeling behind me.

I do as he asks, realising I'm pretty much putty in his hands. I know what is coming and I want his mouth pressed against my sweet spot more than anything else right now. One of his large hands grips my hip whilst the other pushes gently against my lower back urging me to bend over. My body follows his demands instinctively.

As the water pours over my skin, Bryce's mouth presses against my clit, his tongue swirls there, the pressure just right. I bite out a moan, my fingers curling against the tiles as his lips slide over the sleekness of my opening. Then he licks me firmly, front to back, back to front, repeating the movement over and over, only pausing to press his mouth firmly against my clit or to dip his tongue inside me. My legs begin to shake, as my orgasm builds. He is relentless, he doesn't allow me a moment to relax, to catch my breath. I am as tight as a drum, wound up with need and want. Then, as though he knows exactly what I need right at the point I need it, Bryce slips two fingers inside me, curling them just at the right spot and I explode with a loud scream as the most intense orgasm rips through me. I ride the wave whilst stars splinter behind my eyelids. My hands slide from the tiles as my legs buckle beneath me. Bryce catches me as I fall, burying his head into my hair as tears roll down my cheeks with the intensity of my orgasm and the new overwhelming emotions I am beginning to feel. I remain like that, curled in his arms at the bottom of the shower, for some time. He doesn't try to move, he simply cradles me against his chest, the sound of his heart beating loud in my ear.

EIGHTEEN

As I pull on a pair of jeans and turtle-neck sweater, I think back on what's just happened. Sex with past boyfriends had always been about them, not once had they made sure I was satisfied. The orgasms Bryce and I had experienced were intense for both of us, but that isn't the part that makes my heart ache the most. It's the way Bryce held me after. No man before the brothers Freed has ever held me that way. All sorts of strange emotions are running through me, emotions that are alien, that I'm not ready to feel. I grab the hairdryer from the side table and tip my head forward, blowing the hot air over the strands that fall in front of my face, trying in vain to distract myself. These are dangerous thoughts. I must protect myself, and yet I keep letting them in. I'm clearly a glutton for punishment.

"Louisa," a voice says over the sound of the hair dryer. I almost jump out of my skin. I flick the switch off and turn to find Max staring at me. His cheeks are bright red from being in the cold. "Do you need a hand?" he asks, pointing to the hairdryer.

"It's fine. I can do it," I say.

He sighs, running a hand through his hair. "What I meant to say was, can I do it, can I dry your hair?"

I remember what he said about his mum before, that he used to brush her hair for her, that those were his fondest memories when everything else was pain and heartache. For whatever reason, he needs to do this for me. What would it hurt if I let him?

"Sure," I say, finally.

Max takes the dryer from my hands and slides behind me on the edge of the bed, his thighs pressed against the outside of mine. He runs his fingers through my hair as he dries it, making sure that the hot air doesn't get too close to my skin. Like before he is gentle, his fingers massage my scalp as he dries it. I feel my body relax against him, enjoying the sensation.

It doesn't take long until my hair is completely dry. I'm kind of sad about it. It feels nice to have him take care of me this way. Without saying a word, Max flicks off the hairdryer and lays it on the bed, picking up my hairbrush.

"Is this okay?" he asks.

"Uh huh," I mumble as he runs his fingers over my scalp.

"You have the most beautiful hair, it's like silk."

"Thank you."

For a long time, he pulls the brush through my hair, taking his time to get out the knots. A strange kind of tension fills the air. It is not sexual, more like something bonding between us. I don't know, I can't explain it.

"Believe it or not, I'm pretty good at a French plait. Would you mind if…"

"Sure," I say quickly. To be perfectly honest, I want to explore what is happening and don't want to break the spell that seems to have settled over us both.

Max's fingers work their way expertly through my hair. He gathers a small section at the top, then works his way down, pulling up strands and plaiting them. Eventually his fingers trail over the nape of my neck.

"Do you have a band?" he asks.

"Yes, in my wash bag. I'll grab one."

"It's okay, let me." Max hands me the end of my hair to hold onto. Then he clambers off the bed and grabs a hairband. I look up at him as he approaches. He is smiling happily as he ties the band over the end of my hair.

"Not bad, even if I do say so myself," he grins, pulling me up. He presses a sweet kiss against my lips and pulls me in for a hug. He holds me there for some time.

"Thank you," he says, before pulling away.

"For what?"

"For being you, for letting us in. I've got a good life now. It's even better now you're in it."

"I don't know what to say..." My voice trails off.

"You don't need to say anything. Just know you've made quite an impact on us all. Come on, Hud and Bryce want to play some games. Believe me you don't want to miss this."

"Games? What kind of games?" My mind goes to a naughty place, and my cheeks flush a little at the thought.

Max bursts out laughing. "Not those kinds of games, Icy. I'm talking about Monopoly, Cluedo. If you're lucky, they might even insist on Charades. Although, I don't think they'd take much persuading to play the games you're thinking of," he says with a wink.

"Ha ha," I laugh.

Max takes my hand and pulls me around the bed and out of the room.

"You're such a cheat!" Bryce complains, giving Hudson a look of disgust. "I knew we should have given Louisa the job of banker. You've been nicking money, haven't you?"

"I don't know what you're talking about," Hudson responds, feigning innocence. "Just because I'm a better businessman than you, there's no need to cast aspersions."

"Erm, Hudson, Bryce is right, you've been pilfering money since the start," I say, leaning behind him and pulling a wad of bank notes from his back pocket. I wave them in the air.

Hudson snatches the money from me with a laugh.

"You got me."

"Whaaaat!" Max throws his hands up in the air in mock disgust. "The banker wanker strikes again."

"Banker wanker?" I giggle. I've never heard that turn of phrase before and it's made even funnier hearing Max say it about Hudson. "You guys are adorable," I say, before I can stop myself.

"Adorable, eh? I'm not sure adorable is the best adjective to describe my brother. Frankly, wanker suits him better," Bryce grumbles.

"Oy, sore loser, enough of the wanker," Hudson says, chucking the money at Bryce. The notes flutter to the floor.

Bryce raises his eyebrows, smirking. "This is not fifty-two card pick up, I'm not falling for that again." With that he gets up and heads into the kitchen. "I fancy a beer, does anyone else want a drink?"

Max starts to put the game away. I help him.

"A beer for me too, Bryce" Max responds.

"I'll have a glass of red. Louisa, would you like something?" Hudson asks me.

I don't normally drink. For obvious reasons, Mum has put me off alcohol, but it is Christmas and one wouldn't hurt. "Sure, a glass of red wine would be lovely," I say. I haven't actually drunk red wine much, but before Richard realised just quite how bad my mum's alcoholism was, red wine had been their drink of choice. Somehow it reminds me of him, and happier times. Back then, she had almost beaten her addiction.

"Coming up," Bryce says. "Hey, Max, give us a hand with some nibbles. I'm already hungry again."

"Sure," Max says, getting up, leaving Hudson and me to tidy up the board games.

Behind us Max and Bryce discuss what they are going to serve up, leaving me alone with Hudson. I'm not particularly hungry, full still from the huge Christmas dinner I consumed earlier. But these guys are always eating. I have no idea why they aren't overweight beasts but then, given their physiques, they aren't exactly strangers to exercise.

"Louisa," Hudson says, placing his hand on top of my own.

"Hmm?"

"Earlier, when Bryce said what he did…"

I sit back on my haunches, pulling my hand out from underneath his. "You don't have to explain anything. I'm fine, honestly," I say. He really has no need to justify his way of life to me. I have no claim over him.

Hudson ignores me. Apparently, sharing his thoughts is his aim, and he isn't about to stop.

"He wasn't lying. That's exactly how I led my life. Working hard, then fucking. Pretty much that, repeatedly. It prevented me from really considering stuff."

"Stuff?" I search his face and wait.

Hudson sighs. "Why I am the way I am. I mean, I know why, I just never wanted to figure it all out before. To heal, is what I'm trying to say. I was happy with my life. Work kept me busy and fucking kept my past at bay. It temporarily filled a hole."

"And you aren't happy now?" I ask, frowning.

He bites at his fingernail. "No, I mean, yes, I am. I'm proud of the business I've built, *we've* built. I love my brothers even when they act like dicks most of the time," he says, glancing at them, a smile pulling at his lips.

"But?"

"Something is changing. I have no fucking clue whether it is a good or a bad thing, but I want to try and figure my shit out once and for all. When I get home, I'll be hooking up with my shrink again. I *want* to be a better version of myself. It's about fucking time, to be honest."

"I'm happy for you," I say, and I am. To talk about healing is one thing, but to actively seek it out despite the

140

pain he will inevitably go through, is quite another. I place the board back in the box and slip on the lid. I move to stand but Hudson stops me, placing his hand on my arm.

"I'm sorry if what you heard earlier upset you. You are part of the reason I want to change, Louisa." He says it so softly that I'm not quite certain I heard him correctly, but I don't get a chance to ask him to repeat himself as Bryce and Max join us once again.

Hudson lets go of my arm and grabs the bottle of red wine from Max, pouring us both a glass. I take the one he offers me.

"Thanks."

He nods his head and takes a sip, peering at me over the rim of his glass. He's looking at me strangely, like I am an oddity he doesn't quite know how to figure out. I turn away from his gaze, uncertain how to react under his scrutiny.

"You two alright?" Max asks, noticing the strange look Hudson is giving me.

"Never better," Hudson says, taking a seat on the sofa.

Bryce places a selection of cheese and biscuits on the table, a plate full of sliced meat, and a bunch of grapes. Max adds plates and cutlery.

"Figured we could just eat this here," he says with a shrug. "Help yourself."

Max sits on the floor by the table and loads his plate with food. Bryce sits on the other side of me.

"What would you like?" Bryce asks, taking a plate.

"Honestly, I'm not that hungry. I'm stuffed from earlier."

Bryce slices a slither of cheese and lifts it to my mouth. "Just try this. It's delicious," he says, his eyes focusing on my lips. I open my mouth and take a bite. It's stronger than I usually like, but it is delicious.

"Good?" he asks.

"It's lovely," I say, following the mouthful with a sip of wine.

Hudson slides to the floor next to me and pulls a grape from the bunch. He places it between his teeth then leans forward. The action makes me giggle nervously.

Fuck it, what does it matter. If Hudson wants to feed me grapes from his own mouth, then who am I to deny him? Leaning over, I bite down on the proffered grape, breaking it in half. Hudson pulls back, chewing his half whilst I do the same. A little bit of grape juice slides down my chin. Hudson wipes at it with his finger. Then he leans in and presses his lips against mine. My mouth parts as his tongue slips inside. He tastes sweet, but his kiss is far from it. *Hungry* comes to mind.

When he pulls back a grin spreads across his face, just as a grape comes flying towards him. He isn't quick enough to react and it bounces off his forehead.

"Why, you little…"

"Bloody hell, Hud. Smooth operator or what?" Max laughs, taking the piss. The grape missile clearly came from him.

Hudson shrugs. "Bryce started it." He looks at me. "I didn't want to miss out."

"Well, I'm pretty sure Louisa is capable of feeding herself," Max retorts with a grin.

"I *liked* it," I say, my own embarrassment making my face flush with heat.

Max turns to me, the smile slipping. In its place, heat sparks in his eyes. "Is that so?"

I don't have time to answer before he jumps up and heads into the kitchen. I watch as he starts pulling items from the fridge: a punnet of red berries, some chocolate mousse, cream, then from the cupboard he pulls a jar of honey and a bar of dark chocolate. He gathers all the items and heads back over to us, placing them all on the table with a wink. Neither Bryce or Hudson say a word as he runs out of the room. A moment later he is back with a piece of black, silk material that looks suspiciously like a blindfold. He runs it over his palm.

"Wanna play?" he asks.

I look at all the items on the table. Then my gaze lifts to Max's expectant one.

What the hell.

"Who's first?" I ask, biting on my lip.

NINETEEN

"Well, darling, you of course," Bryce says, holding his hand out for the blindfold.

Max drops it into his hand and Bryce scoots in closer to me. I turn my back to him, so he can place the blindfold over my eyes. He is exceedingly gentle as he ties it around my face. Once he has done so, I feel a featherlight kiss press against the curve of my neck. I startle at the sensation, my other senses heightened now I've lost my ability to see. Bryce chuckles.

"It might be easier if you sat back on the sofa," he says. I reach my hands down and scoot back, settling into the soft cushions. My heart is already pounding in my chest with the anticipation of what is about to happen next. I hear a jar being opened and the rush of air as someone sits down on the other side of me.

"Open your mouth, Icy." It's Max. His voice is low, seductive and despite the fact he is using my nickname, there is no humour.

I open my mouth and wait, feeling a little uncomfortable

at what I must look like. A gentle hand rests against my cheek as a cold spoon slips past my lips. I close my mouth around it. The sweet taste of honey explodes across my tongue as Max pulls the spoon from my mouth. I swallow, running my tongue over my now parted lips, lapping at the sweet taste. Max's hand slides down my face. The pad of his finger pulls at my bottom lip. I hear him groan as I open my mouth, allowing him access. Closing my mouth over his finger, I suck hard.

"Damn it, Louisa," I hear him say as he shifts closer to me on the sofa. He pulls his finger free, replacing it with his mouth. "That sweet mouth of yours..." he starts, before sliding his lips over mine. He kisses me hungrily, both hands cupping my face. When he pulls away I am left breathless and wanting. I want more of him.

"My turn," Bryce growls. The nuances of his voice have become familiar now, my man-mountain is turned on. So am I. Max moves back as I turn my head towards Bryce. He leans over me and I can feel something firm press against my mouth. It smells like strawberries. He runs it across my lips before sliding it in. I take a bite, a little of the juice runs free. Bryce gives me a moment to swallow then he leans down and licks, *actually licks*, across my lips. I never thought such an action would turn me on so much, but it does.

"Bryce," I whisper when he pulls back. If I sound needy, it's because I am. I want him to kiss me.

He does.

My hands pull on the back of his head, urging him closer. Bryce obliges, going one step further. I feel one arm slide under the back of my knees as his other snakes around my back. He lifts me into his arms and for a long time there is just us as everything else dissolves. Bryce's kiss becomes more heated, urgent, and his hands begin to stray further, moving up my thigh and under my top until they rest against my stomach.

"Bryce," Hudson says. I can barely hear him over the rushing and pulsing in my ears. "Bryce," he repeats. Bryce pulls away, a low chuckle erupting from his chest. "Sorry, Hud. Louisa is…"

"I know, brother, I know," Hudson says.

It is entirely strange to hear them talking about me and not see the expressions on their faces. I feel utterly desired. I am a hot mess in his arms. Bryce presses a kiss against my lips then slides me off his lap and into the arms of Hudson.

"Hello, beautiful," he says, before crashing his lips against mine. I'm not sure what changes in that moment as we kiss, but suddenly I am being lifted from the sofa and carried elsewhere. A moment later I am sitting on something cold and firm. It feels suspiciously like the kitchen table.

"I want to touch you, taste you, not feed you," Hudson laughs, encouraging me to lie down.

I lift my hands up in an attempt to slip the blindfold from my eyes, but Hudson captures my wrists in his hands.

"No, you should leave it on."

I don't resist.

"Lie back, Louisa."

A hand rests on the back of my head and eases me down so that I am lying flat. "There we are, darling," Bryce says. His lips graze across my forehead, before he pulls away.

Warm hands undo my jeans, then roll them down over my

hips, pulling my knickers free too, until I am bare from the waist down. Another set of hands, Hudson's I believe, push my top upwards revealing my lace bra. I lift my arms as he eases it over my head, ensuring the blindfold remains in place. Another set of fingers slide under my back, unhooking my bra. My nipples pebble at the sudden cold.

I hear movement around me, then jump as something cool and wet pours over my stomach, pooling in my belly button. A hot mouth follows the cold as lips move across my skin. A tongue laps at the liquid.

"Hmm, delicious," Max says, pulling back.

The sensations that follow are intense.

Gentle hands slide across my body, soft lips graze across every inch of my skin. Tongues lap, teeth scrape, and moans fill the air. I'm not sure how long I lie there naked and open to the brothers Freed. Time ceases to exist as I allow the sensations to take over. All thoughts of my past, my mum, my self-doubt, it all dissolves under their attention. Nothing enters my head apart from the way they are making me feel. This is all about them worshipping me. Every touch, every kiss heightens the pleasure I feel. It's so overwhelming that I feel tears slip from my eyes. Their hands and mouths fall away.

"Louisa…" Max says gently, wiping at my tears.

I can't explain to them that these tears are not because I am sad, they are because I feel adored. In a moment of clarity, I understand the Freed brothers and their addiction to women and sex. This is the closest I have ever felt to being loved and I don't want it to end. Isn't this what we are all searching for?

"We can stop," Hudson whispers.

"No!" I say, almost panicked. "Don't stop, don't ever stop..." I pull him in for a kiss. I'm surprised at my own desperation. It frightens me.

"Sweetheart, as long as you want us, we'll stay," he says against my mouth.

So, they don't stop.

They set me on fire. They play me like an instrument, each of them an expert at conducting my body. The brothers Freed take their time worshipping me with their hands and their lips. They get to know my body, what I like, what I love, what tips me over the edge, what keeps me hovering on the precipice, and through it all I realise one important thing: that in this moment I am theirs as much as they are mine.

EPILOGUE

For two days straight, I lost myself to the Freed brothers. To their hands, to their mouths, to their lust for me. I couldn't tell you if it was love. At times it felt like it. Felt close to something beautiful, something everlasting. Max kept me laughing, Bryce held me when I cried for the mother I never had, and Hudson listened when I talked about the loneliness of a life spent in a house filled with hateful men and a broken woman. It was magical, it was blissful, and then, it was over.

Once the snowstorm had finally cleared, and the roads were made passable, we made our way back down to the resort. Whether it was because, somehow, we knew another storm was brewing or whether it was because those blissful days *were* just a fantasy we couldn't hold on to, something changed when we pulled up outside the chalet. Reality crept back in and settled amongst the cracks we had only just begun to heal.

All it had taken was one phone call. A phone call that led

to me packing my bags and leaving the Freed brothers in the middle of the night, too afraid to say goodbye.

Now, as I sit here by my mother's lifeless body, crying over a woman who broke my heart, my thoughts return to the three men who, for a brief moment in time, made me feel like I was loved, and I find myself wondering whether the brothers Freed are thinking of me at all.

To be continued…

Books two and three of the Brothers Freed series are available now:
https://books2read.com/StormSeduction
https://books2read.com/DawnOfLove

AUTHOR'S NOTE

Avalanche of Desire was my first foray into contemporary romance. This book first appeared in the Snow & Seduction anthology in 2018. Gosh, I can't believe that was so long ago!

When I started writing about Hudson, Max, Bryce and Louisa, I had no intention of making it into a series, but like all my characters, they somehow worked their way under my skin and I realised I couldn't end their story there. Now they have their own trilogy ready and waiting for you to devour!

And if you enjoy their story, be sure to check out my other series set in the same universe where they make cameos!

Much love,

Bea xoxo

Recommended reading order:

AUTHOR'S NOTE

The Brothers Freed trilogy
Academy of Misfits trilogy
Beyond the Horizon standalone
Academy of Stardom trilogy
Their Obsession Duet
Finding Their Muse series

ABOUT BEA PAIGE

Bea Paige lives a very secretive life in London… She likes red wine and Haribo sweets (preferably together) and occasionally swings around poles when the mood takes her.

Bea loves to write about love and all the different facets of such a powerful emotion. When she's not writing about love and passion, you'll find her reading about it and ugly crying.

Bea is always writing, and new ideas seem to appear at the most unlikely time, like in the shower or when driving her car.

She has lots more books planned,
so be sure to subscribe to her newsletter:
beapaige.co.uk/newsletter-sign-up

Check Be a out on TikTok:
https://www.tiktok.com/@beapaigeauthor

facebook.com/BeaPaigeAuthor

instagram.com/beapaigeauthor

pinterest.com/beapaigeauthor

bookbub.com/authors/bea-paige

ALSO BY BEA PAIGE

#4 Symphony

#5 Finding Their Muse boxset

THE BROTHERS FREED SERIES
(CONTEMPORARY ROMANCE / REVERSE HAREM)

#1 Avalanche of Desire

#2 Storm of Seduction

#3 Dawn of Love

#4 Brothers Freed Boxset

CONTEMPORARY STANDALONES

Beyond the Horizon

THE INFERNAL DESCENT TRILOGY
(CO-WRITTEN WITH SKYE MACKINNON)

#1 Hell's Calling

#2 Hell's Weeping

#3 Hell's Burning

#4 Infernal Descent boxset

Printed in Great Britain
by Amazon